Carl, Willi, and Blanche

Barbara de la Cuesta

Plain View Press
http://plainviewpress.net

3800 N. Lamar, Suite 730-260
Austin, TX 78756

Copyright © 2012 Barbara de la Cuesta All rights reserved under International and Pan-American Copyright Conventions. No part of this book may be reproduced or distributed in any form or by any means, or stored in a data base or retrieval system, without written permission from the author. All rights, including electronic, are reserved by the author and publisher.

ISBN: 978-1-935514-06-0
Library of Congress Control Number: 2011945444

Cover art: Barbara de la Cuesta
Cover design by Sherry L. Pilisko

For Pepe and Denise

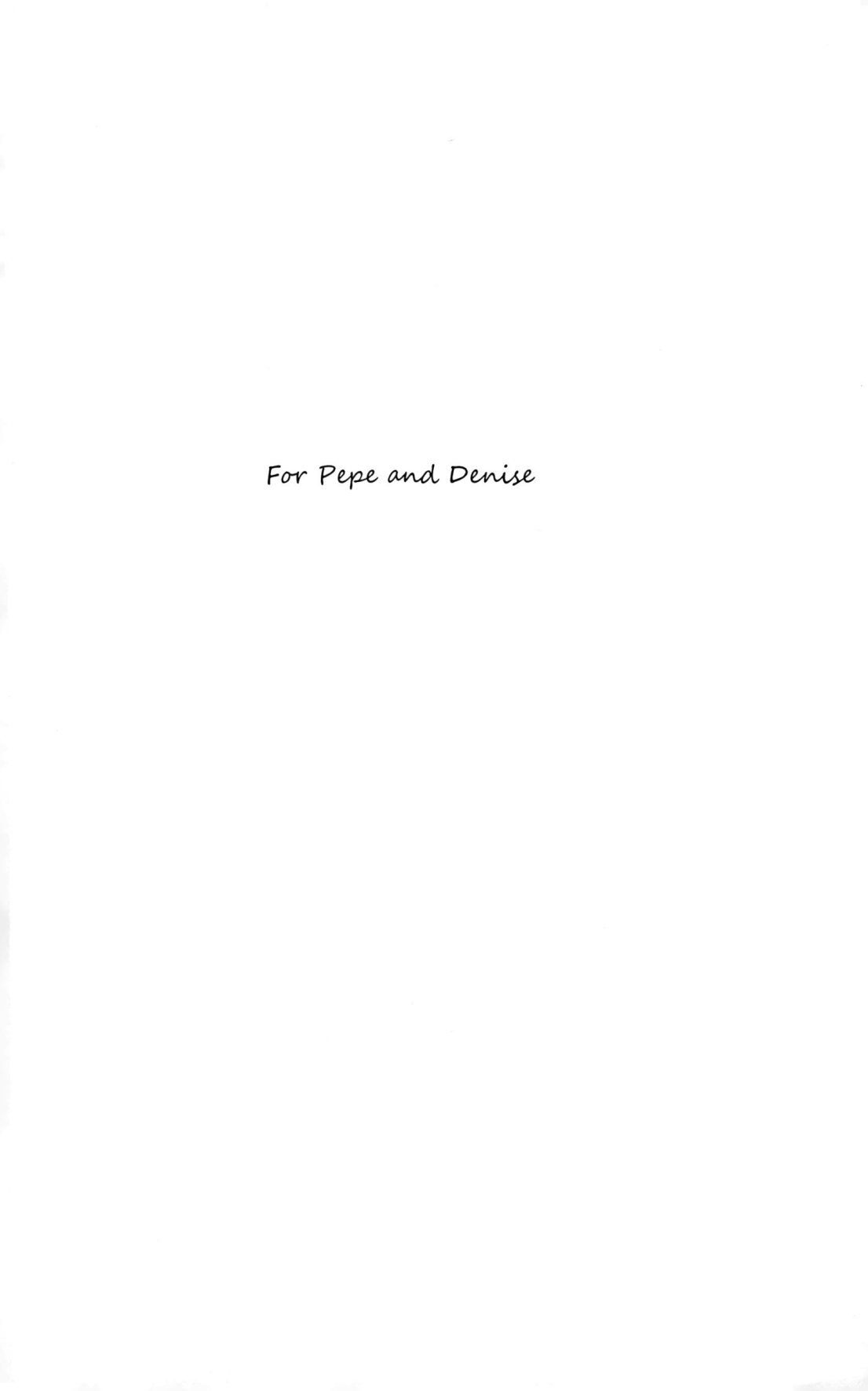

1. Frank Bachelor's House

Chapter 1

It was a portent, of course, that things would turn out differently from their plan.

THEY WERE passing through the small city of Queretaro in central Mexico, and Blanche, at the wheel, had just put the Alberto and Inez tape into the player:

"Alberto presenta a su amiga Clara en el lobby del Hotel:

'Encantadísimo en conocerle,' dice Alberto. 'Les invito a un sorbete.'"

"'Encan ta di si mo!'

"It's the superlative," Carl said. "I am most enchanted…"

"Jesus, Carl, the world is all going to hell and people can still say things like that," Blanche was commenting when she cut a corner too sharply and sideswiped an ancient Pontiac parked near a little plaza.

"Oh, my God!" yelled Willi. Didn't you see it?"

"Yeah, I saw it, Willi. I just still happened to run into it. Look at it; it's a piece of junk." Blanche was laughing, then she was crying.

On the scene immediately was a scruffy soldier; or perhaps he was a policeman; the uniform suggested either. He instructed them to come with him and went round a corner to an armory. There, he took Blanche's license and all of their passports. Then he told them to wait there, and went inside. Willi followed. There was no one at the desk or anywhere else in sight.

They were at lunch, the man said. He took up a post at the door and Willi went back and sat in the car. Suppose they just took off, Carl suggested.

He had their passports and Blanche's license, Willi reminded him.

An hour went by, a good part of another. Blanche didn't think he was really a cop, or a soldier either. But the harm was done.

"If anyone official comes, we can report him," Carl said, but Willi reminded him the man had seen the accident.

Barbara de la Cuesta

Then a well-dressed man came out of the café, and introduced himself as Sr. Areategui and told them they must pay the man something.

"A very old car," Willi argued. "Many scratches already."

"Five hundred dollars should be enough," said Sr. Areátegui.

"Dollars!" laughed Blanche." Dollars!"

"I'm afraid so. It is unfortunate."

"Damned unfortunate," said Willi. Carl fished in the backpacks and came up with the money in tens and twenties. It was more than half of the money they had saved since the previous January.

THEY SLEPT under the stars that night, saving on hotels. Carl lay awake listening to the farm animals stamp their feet in a nearby stable. They were almost fifteen hndred miles from home, from the duplex on Chicago's west side, from his childhood bedroom where a month ago he had lain on his narrow bunk bed with Blanche listening to the Alberto and Inez tapes, from the little Congregational college founded by his grandfather where all Browns studied, from the Art Institute where he had met Willi, from the upstairs room with the rooting begonias where he and Willi drank beer and listened to Fidel Castro on short wave.

Here are, the three of us, he thought, who didn't even know each other a year ago, Carl Brown, Blanche Bell, Willi Ott, on the road in Willi's twelve year old Buick. Going to crash with an uncle of Willi's who owned a sausage factory in Salvador.

Blanche, who it must be admitted was simply along for the ride, lay next to him in her sleeping bag. Actually, her bag was spread open because of the heat. Blanche, who had been on the road since she was sixteen and whose last residence before Carl's bedroom had been Boston Common, felt easy under the stars and wanted him to make love to her, but Carl felt too exposed in this field with the cattle stamping nearby. Willi was quite angry with her on this night because of the accident, but chiefly because Blanche had laughed about it. Carl understood her laughter as more of a nervous habit than what Willi considered her making light of most everything in the world. It was a kind of dissolution, her laugh. But he also felt a little sore. Finally she fell asleep.

He, however, couldn't turn off his thoughts and kept shining the flashlight on his watch as the hours went by.

The farm in El Salvado—besides the sausage factory Willi's uncle raised honeybees and anthuriums—was a little harder to believe in lying here in this field than it had been in Willi's upstairs room. In his night thoughts Carl began to doubt they would ever reach that destination, more than a five hundred miles from where they were sleeping. Their manner of traveling left them too open to interventions of fate, like today's bit of bad luck. Of course the next bit of luck could be a bit better. Luck was a lady, he'd heard. When he wasn't so sore at her, he could acknowledge that the dismal years in the duplex after his father left them, the years his mother sobs were audible in the night through the thin walls, had been suddenly lightened with the advent of Blanche, like a summer storm. Something good could happen next.

Yes, luck was a lady. He couldn't know that the Buick would make their next decision, breaking down a country short of their destination. Or that his next bit of luck was to be a lady named doña Luz.

Chapter 2

Two days later and just over another border, the Buick stalled at a light and wouldn't start.

They had just entered the ragged outskirts of a small city called Las Marias, and were surrounded by juice vendors, billiard parlors, and body shops.

A crowd gathered, children and men." It's the generator. See the light," said a deep voiced child, looking it at the dashboard.

"Lord, that's what it is," admitted Willi." I didn't notice it. Is there a shop around?"

"Yes, a shop," said the competent child. He consulted three men eating tortillas on their lunch break, returned:" *Le empujamos.*"

The four of them pushed; a number of boys and a popsicle vendor on this three-wheeled bike followed. There was a *taller* just three blocks ahead, beside a Lux Cola plant.

"Do we have a part in the trunk?" Carl asked. They had brought some extra parts.

"No, damn! no!" Willi said.

Carl, who spoke best, followed the mechanic. The repair would take five days. They could get back to the *pensión* in town on the blue and silver bus line.

"How much?" Willi asked.

"I didn't ask."

The mechanic came after them as they were crossing the street:" Wait here is another *mister*. He take you back."

"Hi, ya." A thin-faced man in a red and black flannel leaned out the window of an old gray Renault." Get in." He pulled to the curb, leaned

11

back over the seat and opened the back door with a screwdriver. Willi got in front, Carl and Blanche in back.

"My name's Frank Bachelor. You folks from the school?"

"No, we just came."

"Oh, we were expecting a family end of the month. To finish out the term."

"What term are you talking about?"

"Well, Campo Alegre, the American School. So you're not from around here?"

"No, stuck here," Willi said. "The generator went."

"Oh, bad! Where were you going?"

"Salvador."

"Oh hey! We spent the summer near there, in La Riña. That was a great place. I was going to teach radio repair at the trade school; but Rainey, my wife, had to be here for the baby. We have Rh factor. We thought they could take care of it here, changing the blood; but they botched it and the baby died. Most of the American wives go back to Houston, even for normal births. Rainey's upset. We're leaving end of the month."

"What American wives are you talking about?" Carl asked.

"The American companies."

"What American companies?" It had never occurred to him to expect other North Americans here.

"Celanese, Borden, a few at the air force base. They support the school."

"My God!"

"Well, it's just as well. Thing is, we have three kids, and even though I'm earning dollars not pesos, my salary doesn't reach. It's only two thousand five hundred a year. That's O.K. for a single girl comes here for an experience. We made out when Rainey was teaching too; but with maids walking out on us in the middle of breakfast, things like that; and another of them losing Franky, my littlest, in the market ... Rainey had to quit. Then the baby. She's upset, as I said. You can't blame her. But, I don't know, I was damned happy here, especially in La Riña. I really wanted to teach at the Tech. It would have been really *doing* something. The salary was peanuts, but you live cheaper.

But four kids we got."

"What are you going to do?"

"We're going back. We're going to live with Rainey's parents in Radley, Missouri. I've got a job as TV repairman. In the summer I'll start my Master's at the University. We're here on a two-year contract. I hate breaking it, but we depended on us both teaching, so...When is your car ready?"

"Not for five days."

"Hey, that's too bad. You can stay with us if you want. You can even have our house permanent; we had a two year lease, up next August, and we can't find anyone to sublet...It's ours, paid for through August. You want it?"

Willi laughed: "You got a job to go with it?"

"Well, there was a social studies teacher supposed to show up last week and no sign of her."

"We haven't got teaching certificates."

"Native English is about all you need here. When the dysentery hits, or hepatitis, they fill in with school secretaries, Spanish teachers, housewives, anyone."

DOWNTOWN LAS MARIAS came to an end at a small brown river bridged by a concrete arch painted yellow and terracotta. The opposite bank was lined by large suburban houses.

"Santa Rita over there," Frank said. Most of the North Americans live there."

On the slopes above were pitched hundreds of zinc-roofed shacks. A few large tile-roofed country homes lay off to the south of them. Beyond the waterworks was a lovely green park with breadfruit trees. Frank backed up a steep unpaved road.

"Miguelito only makes it in reverse," he explained.

When he stopped under an umbrella-shaped tree in the flat clearing at the top of the hill, nearly ten ragged urchins immediately gathered around the car.

"Wash it Mister?"

"Not today," Frank said. *Lávame* was written in the dust of both car doors.

A row of mud shacks faced on the dusty courtyard formed by the widening of the road. In the center of them was a large, two-storied house, its first floor painted red, the second, yellow. Frank pointed to it: "We live there. Got it cheap. It hadn't been rented in two years. Too far from town. It's why we couldn't sublet. Neighborhood's bad too." The car washing children—they looked no more than toddlers to Carl—moved with him across the courtyard to the door of the yellow-red house:" Your Missus not here," they told him. "She went out to the store." A large dog bounded out as soon as the door was unlocked, scattered the children.

The first floor of the concrete house, built into the hillside, included an open garage, occupied by a *pasteleria*; and a dark subterranean room, empty. Inside the front door a stairway led up to the living quarters above. The children reconvened in the entryway:

"Can Francisco come out?"

The little boy was already waiting on the landing above. Frank took a basket from a row of pegs at the bottom of the stairs, gave it to him: "Bring us three *Polares* and six French rolls, and get the dog in."

"Can I stay out and play after?" Francisco asked.

"Yes. First say hello to my friends. This is my son Franky. He's Francisco to these friends who are so indispensable to him." They climbed the stair, which spiraled rather grandly to the main floor over the garages. Rainey doesn't like him to play with these kids. I don't see the harm. Only vice they've taught him so far is to urinate behind trees. I don't know… I think that's a healthy thing, mentally and physically, in this climate." Frank laughed. "We call those kids out there our press corps. They wait all day to get a glimpse of us going in or out. God! And if we have a visit…! I don't know what they did with themselves before we moved here."

The door banged below: "Here comes the Missus!" shouted the press corps." She bought bananas at Lino's. "She says they are bananas, but they are *plátanos*! "The Missus don't know what's *plátanos* and what's bananas!" "Hey, Francisco, your mama don't know what's a banana and what's a… Francisco, tell your mama that there's visitors. Two misters!" The shouts drowned out the dog's barking.

Frank's wife slammed the door on the uproar, came up the grand stairway. She was pretty despite her faded freckles, poor posture. Frank took the basket from her, introduced them: "They're from Chicago. How about it! Just came here. Nothing to do with the school."

Rainey, friendly, smiled calmly: "Go on out to the patio with Frank. I'll bring lunch as soon as I feed the kids."

Frank wanted to show them the house. "It's crazy. You'll see."

The stairway emerged into a courtyard, paved in terra cotta tile, whitened by rain spatters. In its center, under a patch of enameled blue sky, was a monumental cube, faced in green and yellow tile, topped by another smaller cube, topped by still another. Built into the lower cube were two glass-fronted cabinets and a small sink. The upmost tier formed a niche with a plaster Stella Maris. The wedding cake," said Frank. "It's a combination bar and altar. Actually I keep my textbooks in it and Rainey washes the yucca and potatoes in the sink." Three dark bedrooms opened off the court. At the back was a smaller patio, with a poured cement table and benches, a small swimming pool, a patch of fenced-in grass, bordered by roses. "It was the roses made us take the house, and the view."

The back of the house looked over Las Marias. "All that down there is ours too." Frank pointed to a back lot descending in several weed-grown terraces to a wire fence and a pair of out buildings. "We thought we'd do something with it, but never had time. The pool takes a lot of work. We had to caulk it and paint; and it has to be scrubbed out once a week. We all get in there in the buff and slosh the old Clorox around. It's been a great place really."

"Fantastic!" said Willi.

"Italian fellow built it, his villa. Without benefit of architect, as you can see. Sometimes I think we're living in some kind of hallucination!" There was another cement and tile altar in the garden, its niche enshrining a bottle of *Agua Damiana*. He lives in a penthouse downtown now. Press corps down there drove him out, I guess. They stole his chickens, broke his fences, painted *hideputa* on his walls. Rich bastard, owns sixteen laundries, and he won't let us break our lease. Look, here's another bedroom and another bath, and a changing room big enough for a bedroom, except no window. You're welcome to move in right back here, if you want; or you can have the whole place in a month."

Willi was looking around, grinning and nodding, rubbing his palms on his thighs.

"Francisco!" Frank called to the little boy, who had put the basket of Lux Cola on the concrete table. "Now bring us glasses and lemons and the tequila."

"Fantastic," repeated Willi. Really fantastic."

"Yeah, isn't it? Rainey loved the garden. We had to take it. It's all there was. We started thinning out the jungle in back, to see what we had. There's a mango tree. Five or six banana, pineapple, avocados, chirimoya. Press corps gets most of the fruit if you don't watch out; but Rainey keeps the dog back there now, so we did get some mangos this month.

"We're leaving the dog, You wouldn't mind taking her I hope. Anyway, in two months there should be guavas again. It's a fight, though, not only with the press corps, but with the *animalitos*. One suppertime, we were sitting right here, eating with the Esriols—he's a photographer with La Republica. Wife came to teach psychology at the University. Anyhow, a brigade of ants, a kind they call *ñocales*, marched away with a whole bush while we were eating dessert: petals, leaves, everything; left the bare stalks. Rainey sprayed everything we had in the house on them; didn't even slow them down."

"Lord, I'd like to have seen that," said Willi.

Frank's two older children, a boy and a girl, came out in their bathing suits. "Hello, here comes the team. You haven't much time before lunch," Frank called. They began a game of volleyball, up to their necks in the water. "And keep the yelling down," Frank shouted. The smallest boy brought out two bottles and some chunky little glasses." *Gracias*, Francisco," said Frank. "This is Franky, I guess I told you that; girl over there—big as a horse isn't she—is Janey, and the other is Mike. A lot of family for a schoolteacher, right Francisco? So your Mammy bought bananas. Tell her to fry them. We like them that way, don't we?"

"Shall I get mangos Pappy?"

"Ah, yes. We'll have them with our Cruz Verde." Frank poured out four glasses of rum. Carl tasted it, made a face.

"Drink up, man; we've got a broken down car and nine hundred dollars between us," said Willi, tossing off his glass.

"Give thanks for no kids," said Frank. "Listen, stay here. I mean it." Willi slapped his thigh again, looked around the garden in disbelief. Frank refilled glasses. The little boy brought him a small basket filled with mangos which his father began cutting up with a penknife, handing the first piece to Carl:" Suck on this; the Cruz Verde will go down like a dream." Rainey brought out a plate of Italian bread, a bowl of mashed eggplant seasoned with oil and garlic.

"This is terrific stuff," Willi said.

"Rainey learned to make it from my mother. Dip the bread in it, like this. My grandfather had a Greek restaurant in Somerville, Massachusetts. He was a great man. Rainey and I went to an island off Paros on our honeymoon; we ended up staying a year in a house we rented for twenty dollars a month. A great year. Only thing in the house that reminded you were in the Twentieth Century was Rainey's equipment she got from the Margaret Sanger clinic. And that failed us. Janey was born in Athens. They kept Rainey in bed for two whole weeks afterwards; it's just custom, a perfectly normal birth. When she got up she fainted! My Rainey, what a girl! She'd never fainted in her life."

"I remember," said Rainey, "looking out the window at all those red roofs and that strange sky...The next thing I knew I was back in the bed again, flat on my back. A little doctor who could hardly see over the bed was saying, 'Madame must not get up so quickly.'"

Frank laughed." Rainey's a breeder. Schoolteachers shouldn't marry breeders. It's why I think of going somewhere else...some cheaper place to live. I think of my kids going barefoot, learning at home with Rainey. In La Riña you could do it; but, well, she's afraid. She's had too much."

Rainey put a plate of fried bananas and bits of veal on the table. They ate with their fingers, the children taking theirs to eat on the grass. A green parrot with a new, healthy plumage descended from the lemon tree beside the table and climbed to Frank's shoulder, taking the pencil from behind his ear and splitting it with his beak. The bird's circular pupils flashed like semaphores." Roberto is a fine fellow," Frank said. "He's going back with us. Only thing we're taking. No matter how much it costs in bribes and certificates."

"He'd sooner leave me than Roberto," said Rainey.

"Listen," said Frank," Stay. How about it? A rent free house."

"We'd pay something," said Willi.

"No, no, I don't want your money. Don't talk about that yet...You like it here, don't you?"

Willi grinned, scratching his head.

"Good," said Frank "We won't talk any more about it just yet. I just wanted to know if you liked it. Think it over, that's all." He got up from the bench, handed Roberto back into the tree."Hey, we take *siestas*. How about you? It's damn hot at this hour."

"I'll stretch out by the pool if it's all right," Willi said.

"Sure, great. I'll give you a suit. You want a bed, chose any one you like."

CARL LAY DOWN on a cot in the back bedroom. There was a high window opening to the kitchen and a door opening to the patio. He slept. Dreams came. Blanche came in to the room to talk to him the way she had in Chicago after she had quarrels with his cousin John. Though she was engaged to John, whose family lived in the other half of their duplex on Lowell Street, she lay on his bed with her legs apart, telling him how she had spent a summer sleeping in Boston Common while her parents thought she was at a special summer camp for troubled adolescents: expensive but they'd manage..."Put your skirt down," he told her. He woke then and slept again and his mother was in the room. He told her his idea of going with Willi, to the place with the lawns for butterflies and the liquor made from honey and orange peel that made your head buzz, and the mules you could capture and ride up to the top of the mountain.

He woke to wipe his head with the sheet and slept again and Blanche was back:

"Listen, Carl, I didn't know what was real and never would in that nice raised ranch in Laurel Heights." Blanche said and laughed until she cried. A kind of disintegration, her laugh.

And the short wave voice of Fidel Castro on Willi's Telefunken: the care of pigs, the tasseling of corn. In perfectly lucid, to him, Spanish...

Juan y Pablo Llevan un fiambre al Parque del Libertado...

The voices on the Berlitz tape.

"I'm sure that's going to be very useful," said Blanche, starting one of their old stoned conversations." Shall I go with you?"

"Sure, come."

It all happened very slowly. A couple sentences could fill an hour. She picked up his things, his books off the bed. "What's this?""

"Fanshen. It's Willi's. Willi's a Maoist."

"Is a Maoist the same as a Marxist?"

"No. A Maoist bases his revolution on the rural masses. Marx based his on the industrial proletariat. That's why we're going to Salvador, because of the rural masses."

"*Que dia mas encantador,' dice Clara.*"

"What's that mean?" Blanche asked, spreading her legs on his bed.

"What an enchanting day."

"Gawd! I mean the world is crazy, Carl, and people can still say things like that?"

"I guess somewhere people still do," he said out loud and woke.

HE WAS SHIVERING. A breeze was blowing in through the open door over his half-naked body. Just outside the little room, Augustina the maid was hanging some flapping sheets on a clothesline, and talking to someone.

"...*como que te vas a mizuree*, Old Big Beak."

"Aaark! *Mala. En mala hora.*" hallooed the bird, Roberto.

"They could take me. I work. I no sit in a tree and do nothing…"

"Aaark!"

"What you do in Miz ur ee, old Big Beak?" A sheet was snapped angrily." They take me I make myself better. I work in a factory and rent myself a little room. I buy a fur coat to keep myself warm. I make six dollars the hour. How you think you going to keep yourself warm, eh? *Maldito loro*. How you think you keep yourself warm in miz ur ee?"

TUESDAY AFTERNOON, Frank drove them to the shop on the Avenida Quinta. The place was, crowded with cars and parts. They didn't see the Buick anywhere. A different mechanic was working, looked uncomprehending at the mention of a 1959 Buick.

"Green," Willi said. "It stopped out there." He pointed down the street. "They pushed us here. Saturday." The mechanic went behind a disassembled Toyota and brought forth another mechanic.

"Ah, yes. It's outside." He led them out a back door to the muddy lot behind. There it was. "We have not done anything."

"Why not?" yelled Willi.

"You said to us, if we could get an old part…"

"Yes, yes…"

"There were no old parts. To order new costs five thousand pesos and takes four weeks to deliver. We could not order without speaking to you."

"It doesn't sound right, "Frank said. "Ramos knows where I live. Why didn't he send a message?"

The man shrugged. "Maybe he did not think you would know… where was the other, the other…*mister*."

"Where is Ramos?"

"He will be in at noon."

Frank motioned Carl and Will outside: "Listen. I trust Ramos, within reason. He's kept my Renault running, adapted VW parts for it, so it's actually' a better car than it was. But, still, this doesn't sound right; there ought to be a Buick, or at least a G.M. generator out there. We've got to wait till noon anyway; so we can check down the street. Most of the junkyards are in this area."

"Maybe a distributor, not a generator,'" said the first dealer. "And not under three thousand; it wouldn't pay me."

"I'm convinced," said Willi. Let's have a beer and go home. I'll make Ramos a present of the car."

"Hey, hold it! He'll sell the parts in that car for more than you paid for it. I'd like to check the place myself. It's the only way we'll find out for sure about the part."

They checked three lots. Cars, stripped down and intact, were piled three and four high in the narrow lots. Frank, small boned and agile, crawled into every accessible Buick, Chevy, and Olds. Willi, fearing his weight on the upper levels, checked a few cars at the bottom. "Nothing." O.K." said Frank after two hours of searching." We'll have that beer now." It was nearing noon. In front of the Lux Cola factory, they found a kiosk beginning to fill. A dusty wind blew through. "Got a refrigerator here?" Frank asked.

"Beer's cold," said the attendant, and it was. They ordered bottled lemonade for their thirst, then two Polares each.

"I'm thinking," said Frank, "You can do two things. You haven't got the thousand, pesos, right?"

Willi reduced it in his head to dollars.

"Right!"

"Well then you can sell it yourself, for parts. Which might be difficult. You being Gringos and all, ha ha!"

"Yeah..."

"It's, it's less the language than the rosy...the rosy cheeks." Frank laughed.

"Ha, ha," said Willi. Spare the compliments."

"Face it," said Frank. "They'd cheat you. And, well, me, they'd cheat, all of them, except maybe Ramos. So, the practical thing you could do is try to sell it to Ramos. But for a good price, or..."

"Or what?"

"Or sell it to me. That is... I can't buy it outright, but I can pay the five thousand Ramos wants—actually, I think he'd take four. Then you take the Renault, with all its. beautiful VW accessories, that you have to take up the hill in reverse; and in a couple years, you see, you see if you can make it to Radley, Missouri in it and we'll switch back, with maybe a few financial arrangements to suit Rainey. As for me, I'll take a clear exchange and forget who's beholden.

"Thing is, my kids don't fit in the Renault. They were smaller when we came. Actually, we came on the bus, and I just bought Miguelito to get Rainey and me to school. We squeezed in for weekend trips, but it was

Carl, Willi, and Blanche

damned uncomfortable. Well, we could take the bus again, but Rainey's had a hard time. I'd like to take her home in comfort; and there's Roberto.

"I admit it's a damned rotten car. I don't think anyone's anyone ever made a worse car than that Renault, and once you're across the border nobody'll repair it for you. It will be pure junk you'll have to pay to haul away. But Ramos can set it up for a couple of year's dependable running, I really think."

"You got a deal," said Willi.

"Well, Wait, man, you can think it over a day or two. I think we both ought to. I mean first I thought you'd be owing me money, then I got to thinking I'd be owing you. We got to figure it out calmly... take a day or two..."

"No, it's a good idea. You got the money right away?"

"Yeah, I think so."

"Good, let's go order the part."

"*Hombre*, you got me flustered." Frank said. "I...I don't like to think of you backing up that hill with all the press corps splitting their sides..."

"You talk like no-good business man."

"No, well, I never said I was a good one. It would be great for Rainey. The Buick... And for Roberto. Well, listen. I throw in the house. O.K.? Till September, rent-free. That makes me feel better."

"No-good bargainer. Let me get Ramos down to eight-fifty," Willi said. "I don't trust you for that. I can do it, O.K. I can do it with infinitives! What do you think?"

"I think yes."

"Let's go, then. We to pay four grand. You not to cheat us, Ramos, old *hideputa!*"

"*Hombre*, you are a man to do business with! We do it! You take the house you hear, and the rent thrown in until September. The mangos will ripen again in another month and then in three months the chirimoyas. Wait'll you see the harvest. And I get the Buick, and to take Rainey back in comfort. So, in a year, we'll talk and find out whose beholden, if that's possible, *hombre*, if that's possible...."

SO THEY STAYED. Getting jobs wouldn't be easy, Frank warned. For every unskilled job, there were hundreds of unemployed natives. They started with the U.S. companies. Willi, who'd spent a summer boning chickens, got a foreman's job at a canning plant. He had to take a native salary, and found

21

most of his time taken up sending daily reports to a Mr. Harris in Portland, Maine about the greasy state of the floors, the lack of paper towels in the men's john. It was being nowhere.

An afternoon, passing a print shop, he saw they still used an old Chandler Price letterpress of the type his father used to have in the cellar to print wedding napkins and business cards.

He knew everything about that press, make-ready, feeding.

"Half a native salary..." He offered himself.

But this just embarrassed them.

Besides they didn't need. anyone. Still, he hung around.

"Pay me whatever you can, 'and I can show you how to make another guidepin out of tin, and your belt there needs dressing,"

So they took him. Carl couldn't believe such a subtle end had been attained with the few broad swipes of Spanish Willi possessed.

CARL'S SPANISH was another matter. He bought a novel every other day in the Libreria Central, starting with the illustrated *Fotonovelas* with their speech balloons, and progressing to poets, Vallejo, Páez, Rubén Darío—reading at the cement table on the patio, afternoons. Mornings, he inquired about jobs without success. He hadn't any skills to offer the American companies, and they were suspicious of him—what was he doing here? It left the school, which held out a promise of something temporary later.

"FEELS LIKE A SUBWAY," Blanche said, waking a morning before six. "Is there a subway here?" She giggled.

"Earthquake!" yelled Frank in the front bedroom. "Earthquake, all out!" He was standing in the center of the patio, as children carrying blankets and pillows went by, waving his arms, directing traffic. "Out in the street. Out in the street. This is a heavy tile roof, and if it comes down..."

There was another tremor. Dishes fell out of the dining room cupboard. It sounded like a train passing. "Hurry up now. Hurry up now," Frank yelled good-humoredly. Augustina, who'd already been up, grinding the corn *masa*, cowered in the doorway of. the kitchen: "*Ave Maria, ave Maria purisima!*" A pot fell onto the stove; some tiles fell out of the altar.

"Out!" Frank yelled at her. "Out!" She wouldn't move. Willi took her by the hand and pulled her down the stairs. In the street below, the press corps was whooping about. A sign had fallen off the *panaderia* on the corner. The inhabitants of the house next door were in the street in their nightclothes. *Ave Maria, ave Maria purisima,*" Augustina crossed herself and knelt in the red dust. Another tremor, rumbled up from the waterworks. Then it was over.

"Wow!" Willi said. Frank examined the walls. There was a vertical fault in the brickwork, visible where the stucco had fallen off, as if the right side of the facade had sunk slightly. "Get out the old plaster bucket," Frank said.

"You just cover it up?" asked Willi.

"What else. The structure's sound. Guadua poles hold up the roof. They flex, and the wood floor too. The plaster is just frosting on the cake."

They went back in, Rainey carrying little Mike, who was crying. Augustina swept up the fallen plaster, some broken dishes. Frank got out a bucket of grout and started sticking back the tiles fallen from the altar. "Fix it right away," Frank said. "Prevents the earthquake neurosis. You can't let them unnerve you."

Rainey brought coffee, scrambled eggs. They ate in the open, on the back patio. The children walked about with their pillows and blankets in their arms. Little Franky was asleep on the concrete bench.

THE DAYS PASSED. The mangos ripened.

Blanche lay under the mosquito net smoking some stuff Willi bought from an old man at the Cafe de a Media Luna on Calle Septima.

"I'm blue. I can't get high on this stuff."

"Stop then." Carl told her

"I'm blue and I'm hot."

"Think about something else."

"When I'm hot I like to think about being hot."

"All right then thinks about it."

"Hot, hot, hot!" She flopped over on her side. "Do you like me, Carl?"

Carl put down his *fotonovela*. I like you. I love you."

"Better than Linda McWhirter?". Frank had gotten him a little job now, tutoring Linda's little boy who went to the American school. He was delicate after recovering from meningitis and studying at home for the time.

"She interests me. I don't want to sleep with her."

"What interests you?"

"She worries about such funny things, and she's unhappy in her position. I admire her for that." Linda McWhirter, who was the wife of a North American executive, couldn't get used to many things here, with what she considered her falsely exalted position being the wife of a factory manager, having to deal with maid's etcetera.

"I'm unhappy in my position."

"I know."

"But. I'm not interesting."

"You're not like her. You're free to change."

"What do you mean?"

"You could go back"

"Do you want me to?"

"No. I love you."

He worried about her. She didn't fit any of the categories of Las Marias women. North American women had husbands and children and houses in Santa Rita; women of the lowest class worked or were mistresses and whores. She supported idleness well. At the beginning, she tried helping Augustina with the cooking, but didn't know what to do with the unfamiliar foods that the girl brought from the *galeria central*. So Augustina continued to cook for them out of a notebook full of recipes Rainey had translated from *The Joy of Cooking*. *Pollo a la Tocineta*," she would inform them belligerently, plopping down the dish. It reappeared every Monday. Tuesday was *Higado en su nido de papas*," and so on. Augustina, who also washed the clothes in the stone tub at the back, and swabbed the floors, didn't need any instruction in what foreigners liked.

A few of Rainey's acquaintances had tried to be friendly to Blanche, but she didn't seem formed for intimacy with other women.

Willi, who was beginning his life, as he thought of it, as a painter, worked mornings on the terrace, behind the laundry tubs, every morning the same overcoming, the same plunge into work; it was like athletics, you couldn't be flat-footed. He was painting in goache on fiberboard. Blanche posed for him on a tumbled cot where she afterward took her nap, or sitting at the cement table with a rum bottle in front of her, or stretched out under the plantains. He loved the plantains; he'd never painted anything as satisfying as a plantain leaf.

He drew her drowsing on pillows or sitting at the cement table eating an orange. One day she sat on the parapet watching the press corps in the dusty street below. A scruffy man had come along the road from Aguascalientes and sat on a boulder to rest. The press corps pressed around this new interest, which became even more interesting when the man took some coins out of his pocket and laid them on the rock.

"*Ves, que tiene plata.*"

Suddenly he threw the coins, over their heads, across the dusty courtyard. They ran, yelling, to recover them, pushing aside the smaller ones, causing them to scrape their knees. Two boys fought. She watched drowsily thinking, it's spring at home. I'm missing the spring ...Her father, Harry, was locked away for chronic alcoholism. She thought she'd write Harry in his institution. Maybe he'd know where Belle was, her mother...

Again the man threw, this time behind him, down the slope. Again they ran; again, the little ones got nothing; returned, weeping to the man's lap: "*Bobos, tienen que correr,*" he scolded them, pushing them off, trying to make them run. There was another fight, and the loser limped off home. She noted how the cameo blooms, which had come out just the day before, were lying now, ankle deep in the street. Yes, she thought, I'll write Harry.

"It's springtime here too," Carl had said last night when she'd noted the fact of missing it. *Primavera,* it was called. But what was *primavera*? Just some weather the winds brought over the *cordillera*. It was wet; that was *invierno,* winter; or it was dry, summer: the mountains burned, the cameo bloomed; nothing to do with spring, with seedlings in the window, with that tremendous cranking over the whole tremendous machinery that made the sun go down hours later or earlier. Here the sun set every day at six.

She would write Harry.

Again the man threw. Half of the children were in tears, the other half crowing over their mounting stores of *centavos*. Why does he do it? She felt depressed. The man was evil. His money was evil. Where there was hardship he was spreading misery. She scratched a mosquito bite thinking, yes she would write. At least you always knew where Harry was. Last she'd known of Belle she was in St. Louis married to a man who owned a salon for treating baldness; but that marriage, she knew from Harry, was over in 1962. Belle had moved alone to somewhere in the East.

Again the man threw. *Corran babosos,*" he called turning his pockets out. He would have done better buying himself a pair of shoes, she thought noting his flapping soles.

The hair salon husband, unlike poor Harry, had been rich. Maybe Belle had something from him, could spare her something. She'd feel better if she had a bit of money her own.

"*Los grandes quedan con todo!*" wailed a child, throwing herself on the grass under where Blanche sat. Poor child, she thought. What if she were to drop her a coin? But no! It would only make things worse. Such a little girl, with fine features, a fat little belly glimpsed through her torn dress, nice sturdy little legs. I would love a child, she thought. I would adopt one of these if Carl won't let me have one. Then I would be happy. It's what I need to make me happy.

After Willi was finished, she fell asleep in the chaise. Willi, pleased with his morning's work, sweated over his lunch. He shared Augustina's mess of rice and beans, then had a cigar and a short nap before going to the print shop.

"NO SIRVE!" said Zamora. The ink was wrong for the coated paper they were using. Cutting it with linseed oil blurred the photo engraving. "*No importa, no importa.*" It was only a political poster; but Willi wasn't happy, found some dusty cans of ink in the storeroom. They wasted an hour; the cans had no labels. Willi sorted them after a fashion. "*No importa,*" Zamoras reiterated. He found one that served, but it was green. They ran it; Hugo, still faster than Willi, put through three hundred in two hours. Willi took over, ran two hundred. They'd get it done by next afternoon: "*bueno, bueno.*" They cleaned off plate and rollers, covered the wells with a sheet of plastic. He hated cleanup, a job his father used to leave to him. It would be more efficient to run shifts till they were finished, but Zamora liked to close up, roll down the iron grille.

"Pretty, the green," said Zamora, hanging one up:

PROGRESO & EMPLEQ, *Ruiz Nogales.*

Shifty green face. The floor was spread with them. They left and stopped for a Cruz Verde in the cantina at the corner. Zamora talked about the new offset presses. Trouble was the Chandler Price still paid.

"You ever want to sell it, I'll buy it," Willi said.

"What would you do with it?"

"Wood engravings, like the old days."

"No call for it," Zamora said.

Carl, Willi, and Blanche

EVERY DAY was the same as the one before. That was what Willi liked. Only Blanche's poses changed, and his thinking about his line.

A slow line, Willi thought. Thoughtful, hesitant line, dividing Blanche substance from concrete substance, leaf substance. Slow, see what slow can do. Overcome facility. Picasso, overcoming facility all his life. Slow, slow; this side bush, this side girl. He held the crayon in his left hand.

"Why do you look at me like that?" Blanche asked.

His uninstructed left hand. When it gains too much art, he'll hold it in his toes. No shadow, no mass, just this line ..."Can you hold it just another minute." She had a wonderful shape, long necked, long waisted. The shredded banana leaves lifted in the breeze with a leathery sound. The press corps were in the subterranean garage again, shrieking with laughter.

"You like me, Willi?"

"Sure."

"I mean in a certain way."

"I don't like complications."

"There wouldn't have to be. "She hadn't had a period for two months. But that was because of the change of water, she thought. .

Between the two of us we can't make her happy, Willi was thinking.

"Carl never gets back till three."

"I'll take you to the Tertulia for a Cruz Verde."

"All right." She jumped up and put on her skirt.

The Tertulia roared with talk. They took an inside table as the sidewalk tables were filled. Willi was happy. His work that morning felt like victory. Blanche caused stares when she walked in; women didn't come here. Clodo Gomez, whom Will knew from the neighborhood, came and sat with them, bringing his racing paper and spreading it on the table.

"Let me initiate the little Miss. You will see; betting is divine when you put your mind to it. But only the favorites at the start. Start out with the favorites. One must have a system."

"A system, yes," said a man reading at the next table. The Tertulia lent out cheap paperback books::collections of poetry, manuals on hypnotism and sexual techniques, *fotonovelas.*.

Pepe Joroba came in. Pepe Joroba was forty-two years old and had written eighty- three plays. Willi had met him at a party at the print shop, when one of his plays, which they printed for him, came out. Clodo ordered another round of Polares. Sit down, sit down."

Helicopters were overhead; they'd been there since the election weeks ago, but people hardly noticed in this the third week of the counting of election results.

WE REPEAT, WE REPEAT, CITIZENS HAVE NOTHING TO FEAR… FROM THE PROTECTORS OF THE FATHERLAND…

"Someone should write a play about this election," Willi said.

"I think I have," said Pepe Joroba. I wrote a play set in the courtyard of this family works for the electric company. They're all gathered around drinking, listening to the radio night after night, waiting for the election results; because, you see, if the other party gets in the father will lose his job…not set here, of course; here we have the glorious Civil Service."

"Byzantium itself," said Clodo.

"You' re right. But back in '53 everyone was a political appointee. It was worse."

"Shall I put Senador or Miel de Abeja the second race?" asked Blanche.

"One's as bad as the other. Put Mi Colonel."

"Teachers were the ones made all the trouble. The Intellectual Proletariat." said Pepe.

"There's nothing for it but to put the top favorite in the third. The fourth you can play around a little. There's Bizcocho and Cruz Verde."

"The Intellectual Proletariat," went on Pepe. Thin soup that lot. Nothing but chalk dust in their pockets, even today." He ordered another round of Polar Beer.

"What do you say? Gemelo or Papel Sellado in the fifth?" asked Clodo.

"Gemelo," Willi said. He didn't know anything about horseracing, but he liked the name.

"That's the favorite," said Clodo. Gives me four favorites. That's too many. I never put more than three. You put more you divide the pot with fifty thousand other *miserables*."

"Let me choose," Blanche said. He passed her the form: "Bicho looks good."

"O.K," Blanche nodded.

"Bicho it is. The ladies have a gift. I ever tell you I win the *Cinco y Seis* twice? The first time I got so excited I got married and made five children before I came to my senses. Second, I would have won, I should say, but I forgot to file the form, and with only three favorites. I considered shooting myself. Nothing is worse than regret. Don't let anyone tell you otherwise. Ah, well, one lives in hope. I play the lottery too."

A cavalcade of army trucks passed, their tarps flapping like ocean waves.

"Yes, one lives in hope. With the lottery, I have a method. I play the end numbers, regular, each week. That way you are bound to win, one or two hundred pesos a month. The money I win I play on the whole number. One lives in hope, yes! *jugar es divino!*"

CITIZENS SHOULD MAINTAIN CALM...

The voice was overhead again. "Good Lord," Willi said. "I thought it was over."

"It takes at least another week, "said Clodo.

THE AIR FORCES WISH TO ASSURE CITIZENS OF THEIR NEUTRALITY.

"I want another *Cinco y Seis*," Blanche said..

"Allow me," said Clodo Gomez, and, taking a ten-peso bill from his wallet, he sent the shoeshine boy to the corner tobacco store. Blanche tried to pay him but he waved her off

PEOPLE SHOULD REMAIN IN THEIR HOUSES AWAITING THE RESULTS...

"Remain in our houses indeed!" said Clodo

"Yes, this play. I had two endings," said Pepe. I could never decide if I wanted it to end well or bad. One of them was they win...their party wins. The hero will keep his job, so they have this wild final party with fireworks and radios blaring. All on stage. I remember something like it really happened in my neighborhood. Only it was a water commissioner's assistant...lived back of me, kept me awake night after night, en *visperas*.

"The other ending was tragic. Twelve kids and no job. I don't remember which I decided on. I have a difficult time knowing if my muse is tragic or comic."

Willi bought a round, and Blanche filled out another card with no favorites, and they walked back, past the *por puesto* drivers, waiting on the Avenida Sexta for four fares so they could head out full for Rionegro; through the waterworks, and up the long hill home. "I'm going to play the horses every week," Blanche said. Belle would like the idea. She tapped the acacia leaves overhead so that they closed into tiny fists. The city smelled of black beans, a thousand evening meals cooking.

She hadn't had a period for twelve weeks now. Only this funny brown spotting. There was something wrong with her. Maybe it was cancer.

Blanche, Carl thought, desirable Blanche, who'd come to his childhood bed and given herself to him, among his books and model airplanes. He felt her unhappiness.

If they'd been at home would she have long since moved on, hitchhiked on across the country? Here, to behave in her old free and easy way was unthinkable. Here, they lived in the house of a laundry tycoon; he read Linda McWhirter's handsome editions of the classics from Spain and Argentina. They were vaguely upper class, if they could be classified at all. The upper classes, here, however, didn't drop out and employ themselves as gardeners and bricklayers.

"Maybe she should have a child," Willi said. "A child would amuse her."

"What do you think?" Carl asked him.

"I don't think much of the idea, frankly. A child isn't a pet."

"True."

"Do you mean personally...a child of mine, or any, any child?" Willi asked.

"Both."

"Well, personally, I consider I'm the end of my family. I've always felt that. I. was the only one. No sisters and brothers, no first cousins either side. my mother over forty when I was born. An exhausted line. Families die. I've always looked on myself that way, an end...the one to express it all maybe, all the armchairs and china cupboards and pot roasts and cabbage soups...press it all into some kind of shape and make an end...

"And as to *any* child; well, we're an exhausted empire is my opinion, the end of a line. One or two more generations, what do they mean? Better to use the opportunity to protest, make a statement."

CARL ALWAYS asked her if she had her diaphragm in, and usually she did, only now and then, about one night in ten, say, she left it out and lied to him. It was like a recurring need with her, deceiving people. It made life flavorful; taking a chance like this was like playing the lottery. Besides it wasn't much of a risk, she'd thought; she was probably sterile, her mother had a friend who was sterile because of her periods. Blanche's periods were crazy. That summer she lived on White Castle hamburgers they quit completely.

Her last period was somewhere back before they crossed the last border. Blanche tried to remember exactly when, but couldn't. There was only this little brown spotting and one morning a brisk flow into the john, and then nothing. It just stopped.

Then, a Sunday morning she woke with her nightgown soaked, cramps like she had never…

Willi, amazingly, had medical coverage through his job at the printers, so he posed as husband, and called the *Seguros*. A doctor came, said it looked like a miscarriage and sent her to the Clínica Carvajal.

"But weren't you careful?" Willi asked Carl.

"Of course. She has a diaphragm."

They scraped her out and she slept all Friday. When she woke, she found herself in a long ward between a woman with a large smooth baby and a woman with a small wrinkled one. The family of the woman with the large baby camped all around her, eating out of stackable aluminum pans.

Next day, she felt better, and got up to get a closer look at the babies. I had a baby in me all that time, this astonishing thing happened to me and I never once believed in it, she thought. Willi came and held her hand. Carl went out to buy her a raspberry ice.

She tried to ask one of the nursing sisters what the fetus had been.

Un muchachito, she was told, *de cuatro meses*. She had been four months pregnant, and all the time she thought she was sterile.

Well, it didn't matter. Probably she'd never be able to carry a baby more than four months. Belle had known a woman like that.

Chapter 3

They threw a party a week before Frank and Rainey left. Japanese lanterns were strung around the pool. Rainey set all her Greek dips out on the concrete table and Frank and Augustina roasted a goat in the barbeque pit. Mostly it was people from the school who came, along with some Peace Corps people and a couple of teachers from the university.

Carl sat at the edge of the pool with his feet in the water while Blanche swam lazily back and forth, listening to a group of Rainey's friends who had gathered round her:

"…and supermarkets! Not to have to bargain over every squash and grapefruit…that will be a relief…"

"…and not to bring the black berries home wrapped in a banana leaf…"

"I'll probably buy everything I see, at least once," said Rainey.

"And have a washing machine instead of a washerwoman. Your clothes won't miss being slapped on stones. And you won't miss your washerwoman squatting in the middle of the patio and lighting candles to keep off devils…" Heard from the wives. And then, from a group of Peace Corps workers:

"Myth…in the mountain villages a headless horseman is said to be seen at the equinox…"

"…persistent myth in all of it of course. And then there's the influence of Catholicism…"

Frank led someone up to him at that point, and Carl stood to shake hands with an older gentleman wearing a suit and tie:

"Rafael Villegas," Frank said. "His nephew is in my history class."

"*Encantado*, yes," said Sr. Villegas." It is a shame, I admit, that I send my sister's child to your school. He will go to MIT, I hope, and study mining, as I did, and spend his life most likely in a place like Colorado, thus depriving this benighted country further of its professional class; but one must think of the child, yes…

Carl moved with Sr. Villegas over to the back wall of the patio." MIT is a very good school."

"Yes," said Villegas." And there is the Colorado School of Mines. That is my Alma Mater. The Mother of my soul, ha, ha! I was unfortunately brought up to believe these mountains were the Mothers of my Soul…." Sr. Villegas waved his hands off to the north where the *cordillera* glowed lavender in the sunset. "Are you familiar with the Colorado School of Mines?"

"Well, no. I went to a very small church college. It was founded by my ancestors, so I was given a scholarship. I studied literature, things like that."

"Ah, literature." Sr. Villegas put his punch glass down on the parapet with an elegant gesture and accepted a crust spread with *baba ganoush* from Rainey. "My wife is a lover of literature. She reads English. She longs to speak English well. You must meet her."

He gave Carl his card. He was president of Cementos Valle. Perhaps it could be parlayed into a job, he thought, putting it carefully into his wallet.

THERE WERE AFTERSHOCKS for a few weeks. The mountains burned, the soot settling on the white tablecloth of the patio table. The chirimoyas ripened. Augustina taught Blanche to cook rice and to soap their clothes in the cement tub and lay them on the grass in the noonday sun to bleach. When Willi got a little raise, they decided they could keep her on for two days a week, after Frank left.. She could keep her room and work for the neighbors the other five days.

At the end of June the family left in the Buick, the roof piled high with luggage, and with Roberto in his cage. As the car bumped down the hill, the three of them and Augustina leaned over the parapet to wave goodbye.

"They might have taken me," said Augustina.

"They might have taken me."

INSTEAD OF THE BLUE and Silver Bus now, on Thursdays Carl took the Renault along the flat straight road the *urbanización*, where Linda McWhirter lived, passing cane fields and dry meseta where solitary palms stood up like floormops propped to dry in the sun. Chickens crossed the road, pigs. The McWhirters lived in one of only three houses built in the new development.

Henry—they called him Kiki—was a nice child, easy to please and talkative which relieved Carl's nervousness. He kept at the work Carl gave him out of his school texts as long as he was allowed to walk around the room at liberty. Sometimes he beat his head with his fists, or tapped his teeth rapidly while he was thinking; but other than this he seemed normal enough. In the middle of the morning Carl took him out to the fields in back of the house to collect stones, or grasses, or *margarita* buds to use as counters in the math problems. After this, Kiki had his lunch with the maid, Berenguela in the kitchen, and Carl had a sandwich and iced tea on the terrace with Linda.

They talked mainly about Kiki. She told him how bringing up a child filled her sometimes with terror; yet she knew she did it as well as anyone. "It's, just, you make these resolves and sometimes things turn out so queerly."

"How do you mean?" he'd asked.

"Well, for example, I was determined to read to Kiki all the books I loved as a child. My mother found me most of them, the actual books, stored over the garage. But they turned out to be impossible."

"How is that?" He was sitting looking over the fields to the city, his face in the shade of a woodrose vine.

"Well, *Bambi*, for one, is an impossible book! I was embarrassed. And Kiki laughed."

"But what was wrong with it?"

"Well, it's *terribly* written. I mean what kind of child can I have been to have fallen for such nonsense. And *Black Beauty*, *Black Beauty* was the worst! This horse

having all these ridiculous thoughts no horse would ever…and gossiping about people. Well, Kiki wouldn't buy it. How I ever did…."

"I liked it too, I think," Carl said.

"Do you think there's something wrong with Kiki then:"

Carl laughed. "Maybe he's just brighter than we are."

"Oh, he's bright, but sometimes I think he's…uncharitable. I mean I'm not sure I like it in Kiki.

"Oh, it's awful, the responsibility of a child," she added.

Carl thought that what Mrs. McWhirter needed was something to think about besides Kiki. She didn't seem know anyone else in the three houses built so far in the development, and never seemed to go into town.

Blanche continued to be curious about her, perhaps jealous. There was no reason to be, even though Linda MacWhirter could be considered a pretty woman.

CARL ALMOST FORGOT the little business card he'd put in his wallet the night of the farewell party until on his way home after one of his Tuesdays with Kiki, as he put the problematic car through its slippery gears to its maximum speed of forty miles an hour, he noted the dusty factory that he passed and repassed on these trips.

Cementos Valle.

He went out after supper, followed by the press corps, to make the call from a pay phone in the *pasteleria* on the corner of their street.

Don Rafa was pleased to hear from him. His offices were not in the plant but downtown on the Avenida Lugo. Carl must pay him a call.

He went on foot on Monday morning and found the office on the third floor of the Edificio Zacour, which stood up painfully between two bulldozed remains of neighboring buildings that had never been rebuilt following an earthquake in '61. There was a tank at the corner, and a soldier posted in the doorway. The presidential votes were still being counted.

"So, you are a young man who loves literature." *Don* Rafa got up from behind his desk and came around to shake Carl's hand. "I always go at this hour to the café downstairs. You will come?"

The Café Candelaria roared like the surf. The doors to the street were all open, and from a helicopter overhead a voice was broadcast counseling calm: "Calm!" cried *don* Rafa raising a fist.

"A cretin calm. The people is in love with calm. Even the young men. When I think of myself at twenty, at twenty-four, sitting up all night among journalists and desperate men plotting assassinations...You, what do you think of such calm?"

"Well, I'm not too interested in politics," Carl said. "Are things really very dangerous?"

"No, it is merely, if there is a change of government, some workers for the state electric, and so forth, lose their jobs to people of the opposing party. It is simple self-interest. And of course the count takes nearly a month, so during that time everyone sits up all night to worry and dispute. So, you are not interested in politics. What is your interest then? What did you expect to find in this cursed place?"

"I don't know…some space…some…" He thought of the afternoons he spent with Willi in the dark bar on Canning Street, Willi nursing cans of ale and a growing grudge against the country his German Socialist father had chosen to emigrate to in the Forties. Like this café, there were newspapers spread across the tables, and loud talk at the bar. Here it was louder, like the surf.

"Explain it to me. I don't understand." Don Rafa made a gesture toward a waiter, who came and took an order for *café tinto* and *aguardiente* with a dish of limes.

"WELL, MY FRIEND WILLI is looking for what he might call 'real'… real work…I can't explain it very well. And of course he wanted to paint."

"And you?"

He wanted to say that perhaps he was looking for beauty, for goodness…, but it was a much too embarrassing thing to say. He had read a good bit of Tolstoy in the past year, and thought of himself as a type of Levin.

THE PEOPLE MUST AWAIT IN CALM…

The voice from the sky caused the roar to cease.

"Ah, yes! We are to wait calmly with tanks in the streets." jeered don Rafa. Yes, you were saying…."

"Just some space …," Carl struggled with his thought. "Some clarity… to begin my life."

"Some clarity! Ah, dark, dark it would have to be for someone to come here looking for light!" cried *don* Rafa. Aye, I'm an old man…"

THE RESULTS OF TODAY'S ELECTION, WHICH WILL BE ANNOUNCED THE TENTH OF THIS MONTH.

"Not so old I don't remember, no. Once I read poetry. When we were not plotting assassinations we read poets and walked into the streets at dawn, haggard and ecstatic, yes! But then he died in his bed…"

"Who was that?" asked Carl.

"The villain we planned to assassinate…!"

THERE WILL BE NO MILITARY COUP

"Twelve years we talked…Aye, perhaps you are right in not caring. for politics. I had a cousin once, became very rich. He used to say to me, 'What is this running with journalists and going to jail?' 'I love this accursed country,' I said. 'I want to save it.'

"To save it, Oh God! I was twenty-three.

"It doesn't do, perhaps," he went on, waving again for the waiter, "It doesn't do to love an entire people…"

WE REPEAT, NO MILITARY COUP

"Aye, *caray*, these elections. Six weeks to count the ballots. What kind of a country is this? The devil's own. But what was I saying? Ah yes, 'One must learn to love what one possesses,' my cousin told me, 'A wife, a son…' He has five sons. I have none. But his meaning is the same: To love one's own life and want to begin it, as you do." The waiter came with the order. The volume of talk surged to overcome the drone of the helicopter each time it passed overhead.

"He became very rich, this cousin of mine. He put all his sons through university abroad. The last son, I remember, told his father he wished to study law at the Universidad Nacional, that this was a good starting-out point for any career. Well, to this my cousin replied, 'The best starting.' out point, *mi hijo*, the best starting out point is aboard an international flight at Chiapitas International Airport!' How about that, eh?" *Don* Rafa clapped Carl on the shoulder and downed his *café tinto* in one gulp..

THE GOVERNMENT COUNSELS CALM AND PATIENCE…

The helicopter was moving off .to another part of the city.

"Ah yes, calm, calm and patience when it takes a month and a half, the counting! In your country they have the voting machine even in the smallest village. No need to wait with tanks in the streets. No wonder there are plots. So, you are a teacher of English."

"No, no. I just thought your wife would desire some conversation…we might read things and talk about them after."

"Mrs. MacWhirter tells me you are a fine teacher." The fact that don Rafa knew Linda MacWhirter was Carl's first indication of how interwoven was the life of the city.

"She is too kind, but I might help someone, I suppose, to learn English."

"My wife has all her afternoons free. You will come on Friday, yes."

"Yes, yes, I'll be happy to."

"She is an idle woman like them all, but intelligent. She amuses herself with languages. We shall see. I'm quite sure you will serve."

Don Rafa lived in el Barrio Santa Rita and always walked home at nightfall. Carl walked with him up the Calle Quinta, as it was his way home too, and they cut through the water works, climbing the path that circled the treatment plant, and pausing at the top of the hill to look down on Las Marias.

"Used to come up here and fly huge muslin kites shaped like buzzards when I was a boy. When they'd break loose they'd fall into the palms of the Plaza Central…Ah, yes. Just look at all those lights, not a flicker." The sun had just sunk behind the Cordillera Oriental and the lights of San Fernando were winking on. "If you didn't know it was Las Marias you might think it was Paris, as my old friend Feliciano Bustamante used to say, and we'd remember how twenty years ago they hadn't the hydroelectric and all that side was dark.

"Ah, yes. It was Feliciano and I put the power plant in, in 1942, it was. 'Is that San Roque over there?' he'd say.

"'That it is,' I'd say. Used to be the Jesuit seminary was as far as San Roque went .

My wife, Lucita wanted to buy a lot out there in 1950. If I'd bought two or three…be a millionaire today….

"She has a good head for a woman, I have to admit. But then, it could have happened the city spread to the east…God, to think that thirty years ago they had no electric power there's that fellow in Chocó sending up a satellite. Truth. It was in the newspaper. He's made a launching pad of bamboo. Lucita read it. Not going to be able to send it up, though. There's a bunch of women's organizations objecting to the monkey…"

"Monkey…?"

"They wanted to send up a monkey, the poor wretch, but the women's organizations have the monkey *incomunicado* in Los Olmos, and a court order to have the poor fellow undergo a psychiatric examination, hah! hah! It's what happens to the scientific impulse here. Well, you go that way, I go this. Until Friday then."

THE FOLLOWING FRIDAY, Carl followed *don* Rafa's directions to the opposite side of the city. Some large new buildings set well back from the street behind gates housed the Canadian and the Spanish consulates. The Villegas house and some other older houses were halfway up the hill and flush with the street. Backing Miguelito up this hill was a bit more embarrassing than negotiating the hill at home.

An elderly woman opened the door for him. She was not, as Carl thought, a maid, but *don* Rafa's sister. He was led back through a series of rooms to a dark study where doña Luz sat behind a large table. She stood and stretched out both arms to approach him, laying them on his arms to show a certain warmth, but also, he thought, to fend off the habitual double kiss of greeting.

She was a tall fragile woman and, but for a certain haggardness around her eyes, looked to be much younger than her husband.

"I must show you around, the garden…" She spoke and moved a little awkwardly, probably being unused to using English; but opening the doors to the deep garden behind the study and walking onto its paths seemed to restore her to naturalness. They were two people who would not normally meet, he thought, and she was seeking to smooth the way by showing him something she obviously loved.

"My camellias," she said, plucking off dead blossoms here and there from the rectangular beds and cupping them in her large bony hand. They were an extraordinarily deep coral and at the height of their blooming.

"Lovely," Carl said.

"Are they not? It is fine summer for them."

"Summer..?"

"Well, we call the dry season the summer. Winter is when it rains in February and again in October."

"Ah."

Her hand was full of the crumpled blossoms and she laid them on a cement bench. "*Flores marchitas*," she said. "How is it said in English?"

"Withered flowers. It's nicer in Spanish."

She became uneasy under his gaze. "But let us go back. You must see also the library."

They returned to the dark study and when his vision recovered from the intense light of the garden he saw that three walls were lined floor to ceiling with books. They seemed to be in several languages, mostly French. "You must take any book you wish," she said.

"You are very kind."

"Look them over, perhaps you will see something."

There were translations of English authors: Dickens, Thackeray, Fielding, bound in red leather; unbound French classics printed on creamy paper. He noticed Henry Adams' *Mont Saint-Michel and Chartres*, and took this out.

"You must borrow it, "she said.

"I've read it."

"Oh, then perhaps something else."

"No, no, I meant it's one of my favorite books…"

"Ah, so. A friend gave it to me. We saw the cathedrals together. I read some of it. It is difficult."

"We might read it together."

"Yes, yes, I should like it. We can study right here in this room." She drew shut another blind that was allowing a tiny patch of sun on the rug, and turned on a floor lamp.

"You speak English very well," he said.

"Ah, no. I learn only a little with Mrs. Galloway the doctor's wife. She has gone back to Tennessee with her family; so I look for you….."

"Next week, this same day at three thirty I am free," he said.

"That is good."

"I've never taught before."

"But Mrs. McWhirter speaks very well of you."

"She is too kind. You are too kind."

"You will come next week then." She walked him to through an airy dining room to the door. "And you must take the book." He still had the Henry Adams in his hand.

"Tell me," he said. "Have you seen Chartres?"

"Oh, yes, and you?"

"Never."

"You must, some day."

He thought of his new relationship to his country and the improbability of ever traveling anywhere.

"Yes, yes, but tell me," he said, "did you see it first or read the book first?"

"I saw the cathedrals first." She picked some blown peonies out of a bunch on a table beside the door, held them in her hands as she had held the camellias.

"Then you must go back," he said.

"Ah, no…"

"Couldn't you?" He thought of her as rich, free to do as she wished. "No," she said quite finally. "I marry; I come here. This is my life."

"But you have never wished to go again?"

"No," she said. "I have never wished to change what has been." She smiled and gave him her hand. "Until next week, then."

"Yes, yes," he carried off the book.

41

RE-READING THE HENRY ADAMS' MORNINGS on the patio was a new pleasure. The book was bound in leather and had thick creamy pages that had to be opened with his penknife. And no one was going to ask him to write a sophomoric paper on it or ask his callow opinion. He would reread all his college books, he resolved. Here under a woodrose vine. And discuss them in a leisurely, adult way with this woman who had left him with an initial impression of her long stooped body, her deep, slightly haggard eyes, and her bony-cupped hands holding the fading blossoms, *Flores marchitas.*

ONE MORNING, Berenguela came to the McWhirters with a child by the hand. A boy about Kiki's age. This is Ricaurte, she told Carl, but didn't mention his relationship to her. He thought he could be her little brother; Berenguela looked so young, with her horny little pigtails, her pouting face.

Ricaurte sat at the ironing table with Berenguela and Kiki having *pan de queso* after breakfast; and after his morning lesson Kiki was allowed to play and hour with him. "He's Berenguela's son," Linda McWhirter explained, "We never knew anything about him. He lives with her sister in the Barrio Lenin."

"She looks too young to have a son," Carl said.

"She's twenty-four. We only learned it the day the census takers came around. I thought, when Berenguela told us about him, he might be a playmate for Kiki. There are no children for him, living so far out here as we do."

Carl watched them play a game of Kiki's invention in which he was pulled on a braid rug all about the waxed tile floors, and addressed by Ricaurte as "DE King." It was hot; he almost fell asleep in the wrought iron' patio chair. Coming to, he heard his own instructive tones coming from Kiki: the sounds of vowels:

"Ee, say it, ee…"

And Ricaurte: "Ee, ee," whirling about on the patio with his arms straight out.

"That's right, teach him his letters, Kiki," said Linda, who was passing. A bit too enthusiastically, it seemed, for they gave up the game immediately.

"Does Ricaurte have a father?" Kiki asked later.

"Of course, everyone has a father,"

"But his father doesn't own a Unimuck."

"What's a Unimuck?" It sounded to Carl like some sort of Arctic beast.

"A Mercedes truck with a special raised axle. But his father doesn't have one. He's telling you a fib," said Linda McWhirter.

"Maybe his father's a truck driver."

"Well, yes, but he couldn't *own* one."

"I SHOULDN'T HAVE told him the father couldn't own a truck," she said later when she was alone with Carl." I don't like to see him refining an overbearing manner on the child. He has so many advantages, Kiki, and this child has so little. He hasn't even been sent to school. I thought I'd see if I could look into the sisters at Sacred Heart. They take a few charity children. Here I am again feeling responsible for the world, but how can I live in my position, everything seeming ostentatious, our house, our car…? And so isolated. And yet if you do try to cross over, to connect, it seems insincere…I don't know, I don't belong comfortably either side. I mean you can cross over if you want. You're alone, no business, no consulate you're tied to…"

A LETTER CAME from Belle, Blanche's mother. Augustina handed it to her while Blanche posed on the patio. There was a hundred dollar bill wrapped in a pretty hanky.

"She's married again. She lives in New Jersey now," she told Willi, flourishing the bill.

"Don't wiggle so much. "Who's married?"

"Belle, my mother. She says the guy's rich. I can buy hashish from those old men who play dominoes on the balcony of the Café Lux." These old men only took dollars for their wares.

"I only grow it," said Willi. I don't pay for it. Bad for you."

"Why? because it's stronger?"

"Because you pay for it. Hold still and stop talking."

She was quiet; but after a time Willi noted she was weeping.

"Stop crying and we'll go to the Tertulia in an hour. We'll buy a Five and Six card."

She wasn't happy. What did she want? Did she want him to make her happy where Carl couldn't. He knew better than that. She was beautiful lying with just a towel over her, propped against a banana tree.

"Do you like me Willi?"

"I like you. Be quiet now."

"Willi…"

Slow line, Willi thought. Thoughtful, hesitant line, dividing Blanche substance from concrete substance, leaf substance.

"Why do you look at me like that?" Blanche asked.

No shadow, no mass, just this line …"Can you hold it just another minute." She had a wonderful shape, long necked, long waisted, long nosed, thick ivory skin that didn't tan, but didn't burn either.. The shredded banana leaves lifted in the breeze with a leathery sound. The press corps were in the subterranean garage again, shrieking with laughter, and probably smoking. He worried they would burn the house down.

"You like me, Willi?"

"Sure."

"I mean in a certain way."

"I don't like complications."

"There wouldn't have to be."

Between the two of us we can't make her happy, Willi thought again.

"Carl never gets back till three."

"I'll take you to the Tertulia for a Cruz Verde."

"All right." She jumped up and put on her skirt.

"I'm going to play the horses every week," Blanche said. I'll use Belle's money, she thought. Belle would like the idea.

"OVER THE LITTLE CHURCH *at Fenioux on the Charente, is a conical steeple an infidel might adore,*" the Doña read.

"That is very pretty, yes," she said. Carl had brought the Henry Adams back and asked her to read from it out loud so that he could correct her pronunciation.

"This word, 'steeple', I'm not sure. It is *clocher?*"

"Yes, yes," Carl said. "You know French?"

"I study…studied…at the Sacre Coeur. We speak only in French. I say my prayers, still, in French."

"Do you? Say one for me," he blurted.

"I beg your pardon…" she said.

He was embarrassed. He seemed always to tread on some delicate part of her.

She went back to the book and read to the end of the chapter, then with her face clear and composed, she sat very still and recited the Hail Mary in schoolgirl French. Carl wanted to compliment her and thank her, but thought it best to accept the little gift in silence.

The maid brought *petites beurres* and tincture of coffee with boiled milk. She removed the little skin off the milk and poured it into the two cups, adding the coffee. "Yes," she said. "One might never exhaust the topic of cathedrals. You take sugar?"

"No, no sugar."

"In Maizales there is a very large gothic cathedral they never finish," she said; "It is more than thirty years I believe being finish. There is not the money. Maizales is a poor sort of town, and they esteem themselves too much to start such a..."

"Yes, yes," Carl nodded, deciding not to correct her verb.

"When I was a young unmarried woman, I and my sister climb...climbed it, the tower. It was as I remember a true gothic church, not an imitation. I was only a young girl, ignorant of such things, and besides it seem to me..."

"Seemed, he corrected, aware he owed her some sort of lesson.

"Yes, yes, seemed, of course."

"I'm sorry. You are saying something of great interest and I shouldn't have stopped you."

"No, no. I must be corrected."

"But go on, please. It seemed to you..."

"It seemed to me ugly, *desnudo*..."

"Yes, yes, naked."

"Naked, yes; but there was also a feeling of great... *fuerza*...".

"Yes, yes, a force. The stresses coming together. I understand what you are saying."

"When I read Mr. Adams sometimes it comes to my head, that church."

"Yes, yes, unfinished things," he said, "Things that are still being put together, you're right. I remember when I was at school, college, living in a dormitory, there was a boy who played the piano, not very expert, still being finished, as you put it. He was working on a Bach partita..."

"Ah, Bach, yes!"

"He would stop and start and go over parts, building it up, and I used to sit in the recreation room listening. I liked to hear him go over and over it, putting it together."

"True, true! Perhaps it was part of my education that church in Maizales. It is preparing me to see Chartres and I didn't know it," she said.

"Where is it?" he asked. "Might I go?"

"I suppose you might. In any case I am sure it is still unfinished!" She laughed. "It is far from here, nearer Las Brumas."

"What is Las Brumas?"

"It is our property in Tula. "West, on the way to the *sierra*. High. We used to go so we could eat apples and strawberries that will not grow here in the valley. It is always cold, and one gets dizzy. The day we climbed the tower, my sister and I…the altitude of the town, on top the altitude of the tower… We start to laugh and then we cannot have breath at all…two schoolgirls laughing and climbing, Ah…" She shook her head smiling.

"We can talk," he said. "You hear how we can talk!"

"Yes, yes, it is true. But I wish to speak the English properly. You must stop me to correct."

"But not when you are saying certain things… It would be like interrupting your prayer…"

Again, he had crossed a line. She stood. Her face was flushed, a dusky color rising from her throat. "The coffee," she said, bringing the brass cant closer. "We will have it now. And there is a *flan* Luisa has made."

After she had served him she stood with a spatula in her hand and looked at him carefully. "Your mother must miss you," she said.

It was an unexpected question.

"I suppose she does," he said. "Our father walked out on us when I was seven," he told her, then feared he had crossed another line.

"How terrible." She said, looking at him gravely.

"But she's not alone. We live in a duplex next to her sister and my uncle."

"A duplex?"

"That is a double house. One is a mirror image of the other. My cousin's room was on the other side of the wall by my bed. We sent Morse code messages by knocking on the wall."

"Did you always live there?"

"Since my father left."

"Don't you miss your home?"

Carl, Willi, and Blanche

"You mean that duplex?"

"Well yes…"

"I never saw colors, then. It was all gray."

"Can that be so…?"

"It was so." I'm sure they were there. I just never noticed them."

She stood to collect the cups. Had he spooked her again.

"You think I should not have left," he said to return to the intent of her question.

"Oh no, men must be free, I suppose."

"But not women?"

"No, not women."

Driving home he thought about their conversation. He had noted that he was allowed to reveal more than she allowed herself to reveal. He might have even gone on and told her how the first color he saw was the red cover of a copy of Stendhal's *The Red and the Black* when he was a freshman in college.

FERIA BEGAN. The McWhirters gave parties. Berenguela slept in, in order to help with the cleaning. Ricaurte stayed with her three and four days a week, finally came to live altogether, slept with Berenguela in the big bed which had been the cook's, was bathed by her in the laundry tub in the wash patio, set in the sun to dry.

"What do you think of him?" Linda McWhirter asked Carl a morning.

"He seems like a nice child."

"What I mean is I think he's a spook."

"How so?"

"Kiki came to me this morning and asked if he was baptized…that Ricaurte had told him all the children in the Barrio Candelaria who weren't baptized were getting sick and dying…"

"What?"

"I couldn't think what I meant until I looked at the morning paper; he meant vaccinated."

"Does Ricaurte have a father?" Kiki asked Carl while they were at sums.

"I told you, everyone has a father."

"But he doesn't own a motorboat."

"Maybe he's a fisherman."

"Ricaunte says I can ride in the boat. He says we'll go to La Ventura and catch *bagre*."

"You mustn't get so excited."

"I'm not excited. I don't believe him."

Linda brought lemonade out to the patio. "Tell me," she said, "how you find the Señora Villegas? She's rather a mystery to most of us."

"She is very good."

"How do you mean that? I know she's involved in many charities… Perhaps she might know about where I might send this Ricaurte to school."

"I'm sure she would, but I don't think I meant that by saying she's good."
"Really, what then?"

"I couldn't even tell you. And there's this: sometimes she becomes excited by something she is telling me. Like a young girl teasing me with a piece of candy and then I come galumphing after and she'll turn around and look at me as if we hadn't quite been properly introduced."

"But how do you mean that she is 'good.'"

"Well that she is so…modest, so contained, so solitary."

"I hear she's very shy. The women here are very vain and provincial I find. They talk of nothing but their dresses and their servants and their difficult births, or the large numbers of their children. Perhaps she is different. I wish I knew her. What do you talk about?"

"Oh, about gardens, and architecture, and music, sometimes."

"How wonderful. I feel that I should talk about such things and not always about Kiki."

LATER THAT WEEK, sitting on the patio drinking iced tea with Linda McWhirter, Carl heard the matter of the Unimuck renewed.

"He'll let you, I know he will," Ricaurte was saying.

"But suppose he comes in the Toyota?"

"Never mind then. I've ridden in plenty of those."

"I guess there's no worry on the point of Kiki being spooked," said Lennie McWhirter."I'm just as glad not to have to part with either of them. Berenguela's virtues are numerous."

"Are they?"

"Oh, yes. She always remembers to get down the cobwebs on the ceiling, and washes around the light switches and..." Linda McWhirter laughed. "Is this really me talking?" She shook her head. "I mean we've had some girls...there was one threw all the record jackets away. She thought they were disposable. Another kept rearranging the furniture-she liked things catty corner...Oh, dear, how I must sound to you...."

"What do you mean?"

"So...lady of the manor. The fact is I'm uneasy with the whole servant question. I mean one minute I'm too strict and the next too soft. I never know where my responsibilities begin and end. When Berenguela first came, she seemed such a defenseless little thing from Cahuete we wouldn't let her out past ten p.m.; it wasn't till the census takers came around we found she was twenty-four and had this son. It was almost a relief to give up guarding her virtue. Oh, dear...

"It's I have no sense of what's fitting. You know what I did once: We had just arrived and were staying at the consul's house that was empty for the summer; even the housekeeper was gone and had left behind these two kitchen servants to look after us and the rest of the house. We were just going to be there a month while our house was being done over. Anyhow, the housekeeper had left me a note saying she was leaving the two servants 'their bread for the month.'

"I didn't know if she meant literally bread, or *daily bread*, as in 'Give us this day....' I decided the second. I mean why would she only leave literal bread? So, I bought and cooked just for us and left them to themselves. After two weeks, finally, they looked so forlorn I asked them about it. Two weeks, two weeks they'd had nothing but bread. How could I? How could I? Ever since, I've been too much the other way."

"An understandable mistake," Carl said.

"No, no. It was mean. Mean spirited. I'll never forgive myself. I was annoyed that these two women had been left underfoot. I wanted to ignore them, do things my way. I didn't try to understand."

"You tend to paralyze yourself with doubts," he said.

"Do I? Yes, I do!"

He understood her awkwardness with servants, however. The three of them still hadn't figured out how to deal with Augustina. They worried about her every mood and often wished her gone, yet had become dependent on her.

"I never saw you ride in a Toyota." Ricaurte was heard to say.

"You think you see everything I do? I went to Las Tortugas where there, isn't any road, and we stopped by a river that had snakes," said Kiki.

"My father kill a coral and a cascabel and a mapanare! Ricaurte ran in a circle, flapping his arms.

"But listen," Kiki yelled. "You aren't talking about real things."

"Oh, yes I am. Real things. A mapanare bite you and you take two steps and you're dead!"

"I look at Kiki sometimes and I want to apologize for such a mother." said Linda MacWhirter. I remember thinking once when he was little and I was giving him a bath: Oh Kiki, your mother meant once to read all of Proust and she hasn't done it.... I used to think if there was some kind of little Eton suit I could put on him and he'd be safe...

BLANCHE'S MOTHER WROTE. Carl's cousin, who had been Blanche's fiancé, was dead, killed "in a military accident," What was there to say...? Ade under sedation. Franklin, you had to ask him to repeat everything he said, his voice gone so dead.

There'd been three communications: Gravely wounded, the first. Then a visit from a paraplegic in a special van. John was hit in the neck. A quadriplegic. They had to sit and digest that while the paraplegic enthusiastically told them of a friend of his could only move his eyebrows; up for yes, down for no; and still had gone back to college and was president of the student council and edited the college poetry review.

This visit they'd had to endure and two days later learn that he was dead. A blessing, God forgive me," Rika wrote. What bitter times.

And when were they not bitter? For most of his life his mother, and his aunt and sister had been the women he knew. He didn't recall the house where his father had left on a sales call and never returned, but he recalled the day they moved into the narrow duplex on Twelfth Street, next to his aunt and uncle's, walking up the sidewalk behind his sister, carrying boxes, lamps; He overheard his mother's sobs in the night, the details of his aunt's complex illnesses in the kitchen. It reduced him to a craven fear that these women would die of their unhappiness and leave him alone. It lasted right through most of his years at the little church college founded by his grandfather where he commuted by train.

It was a college founded mostly for children of missionaries; and, with its curries eaten cross-legged on the floor at the International Students

Society, it managed a certain universalism while eschewing the worldly; so that he awoke there more slowly then he might have from the anxious sleep of childhood. He remembered a day, lying under a tender green bush with a very plain Iranian maiden he had met at a missionary dinner. They had skipped out on the talk with slides and were reading aloud a novel in French, and suddenly the world changed from black and white to technicolor, just as his mother said the films changed during her lifetime. Then came Willi and he stepped further into color, and then Blanche who came with her flaming rebellion into his childhood bed.

Carl handed the letter to Blanche. She read it and walked into the plantain grove. He let her go and went and got the shears and started pruning back the roses around the pool.

THE DOÑA WAS NOT in the library the following Wednesday when he arrived a little early. Carl went round the shelves again, looking at her books. He was holding the Modern Library volume of The Red and the Black in his hand when she came in from the garden. "This was one of the first colors I saw," he said, showing her the cover, which was not red but a faded black. Perhaps it had always been black. Only the rectangle which held the title was red.

"You must borrow it," she said, refusing to satisfy his desire to engage her deeper interest in him while she set about laying out the notebooks and the pencils and the Henry Adams.

"Oh, you mean the gray. When you were a child," she commented then. "It is a pity. I saw many colors. The margaritas of my mother that grew in our patio. The coffee bushes of Tula. The pines. The eucalyptus. Such a curious blue. I sent away for a reproduction once. 'Blue Horses', it was called. I had it framed and hung it in my bedroom…"

"Yes, yes…"

But that is all she said. The word "bedroom" had spooked her, and she had opened the Henry Adams to the page where they stopped last. She was wearing a very severe dress this afternoon, a jumper that resembled a school uniform and a starched white shirt.

Her sudden changes reminded him of girls he knew in grammar school. Their boldness and then sudden modesty.

As she read, the slight pink color, which had left her face from her boldness, returned to her cheeks and the tip of her nose. She was like the camellias in her coloring, a waxy white tipped with coral, easily bruised. Her reading hesitated and he looked away so that she would continue. But she paused and looked at him. "It is a novel notion."

"What is that?"

"That Chartres should be a playhouse for The Virgin."

"Well Henry Adams was not a Roman Catholic. A Catholic would probably not observe such a thing."

"How is that?"

"Well most Protestants, like Henry Adams, don't know what to make of the Virgin. They've never heard much about her. So they find the ways in which she is worshipped very fanciful and curious. They try to explain it to themselves."

She looked at him uncomprehending. He thought how he might have explained his thought easily to Linda MacWhirter, or to Blanche, even; but would not even wish to bother. It was only this woman he wished to make such hopeless efforts for.

"I have always love the Virgin," she said.

"Loved," he corrected and immediately regretted. For now she would say nothing of her love and went back to her reading.

CARL BEGAN GOING to the central market with Augustina and learned from her how to bargain over fruits at a stall she favored and meats at another. Filling the baskets and loading them into Miguelito, he wondered. at this new life that to Blanche's despair threatened to become settled and domestic. Would they make their longtime home in The Hallucination? Would Willi go on painting Blanche indefinitely under the plantain tree, on the parapet, beside the pool?

Willi was advancing along a visionary route Carl had decided he could not follow. It was why he dropped out of the Art Institute, the decision becoming clear to him a day when he was working on one of his competent life drawings—model receding in strict perspective on the rectangular stand below the green baize folding screen draped with a cloth spotted with what may have been paramecium—and Willi, who was a student instructor, happened by and talked about the space under his drawing of the model's upraised knee, doodling all the while with his charcoal pencil: ship rocking on a wave, horse running on a mountainside. All under a knee.

Would he go on reading the *Doña's* books on the patio, opening the creamy pages with his penknife, leaving furry edges to mark where past reading from future; discussing the imperious Kiki endlessly with Linda, making drowsy love to Blanche in the little room beside the pool; orbiting indefinitely around his three planetary women, Blanche, Linda, the *Doña?*

The chirimoyas ripened and most of them went to the press corps which seemed to have moved under the house permanently to smoke their cigarette butts and eat the stolen fruit. The election was won by the centrist appearing candidate, who according to Willi's friends at the café was a '*Godo* in disguise'. "IA money, CIA money, you can be sure of it," said the playwright, Pepe Joroba. Willi and Blanche won two hundred and fifty pesos on the terminals of the lottery. Then the monsoons, the rains that came after lunch every day, departed and the dry season began. You could see the pale fires on the mountain sides every day, the soot came and settled on the concrete table and floated on the pool.

IN OCTOBER the matter of the Unimuck was resolved…

"My father getting oysters now at Tuxpan," said Ricaurte.

He had on a new pair of blue overalls purchased in the Casa del Pueblo. They tinted an entire wash blue, Linda McWhirter told Carl.

"You see these overalls I got on; man they're what you call attacking overalls. They squirt out the ink like calamares!" Ricaurte slapped his thighs and was off across the field of cane opposite the house. He and Kiki were after catching *turpiales*, which were easy to capture, and *tijeretas*, which weren't. The yellow and brown *turpiales* were so tame they sat on the arms of the patio furniture. Ricaurte was quick at catching them with a hair net of Berenguela's, and a cage in the kitchen was nearly filled with them; but there was no *tijereta*.

Ricaurte was stalking one now, the hair net fixed to a wire hanger at the end of a stick. Kiki followed him with the cage. After a while, however, Kiki gave up and went to sit on the curb.

"What are you just sitting there for, man?" Ricaurte called.

"You aren't going to catch one," said Kiki.

"Who says I'm not?" Ricaurte smacked the cane with the pole. After a time he came over to Kiki'." Hey, man!"

"You know what I get from my grandmother in New York every Christmas?" Kiki said.

"What?"

"Ten dollars. In a check."

"You lucky."

"How many languages do you know?"

"*Hombre*, I know Spanish. What do you think, I'm going to know…?"

"I know two."

A *tijereta* rose out of the grass. Ricaunte pursued, hopelessly. Kiki picked up the cage and went to hang it in the garage. He came out with his father's machete and sat on the curb sharpening it with a file, correctly as he'd been taught, then he put that away and went into the kitchen and came out with a slice of pineapple on a fork, which he sucked slowly, watching Ricaurte's leaps and lunges. When Ricaurte saw the pineapple, he said, "I'll get one too," and went around to the kitchen.

He came back without the pineapple. "Where's my Mama?"

Kiki was listless, biting crescents out of the fruit. "She's not around."

"Where'd you get that then?"

"I cut it myself."

"You did not. Where's my mama?"

"Kiki shrugged. "Maybe she got sick and they took her to the hospital."

"You crazy."

"Maybe she's dead."

"You crazy!"

"Crazy yourself, chasing *tijeretas* with an old hair net!"

Ricaurte went around the house, presumably to have another look in the kitchen. "She's not there," he said when he came back.

"I told you she's not. Listen, you want to know where your mama is, I'll tell you…"

Carl listened, astonished.

"Where is she?"

"She fell in the *guaca*."

The *guaca* was an old Indian grave which had caved in when the lot was bulldozed. A dangerously deep hole was left which was slowly being filled with compost. Kiki was not allowed near it.

"You crazy man."

"I tell you she took the garbage to the *guaca* and she fell in," Kiki said.

Carl got up from where he sat on the patio wall.

"She fell in. She's dead. Your mama's dead."

Carl came around the back of the house in time to see Ricaurte rush like a demon around the side of the house, bash in the screen door, and fall at the feet of Berenguela, who as usual at this hour was chopping onions and tomatoes for the salad. Probably she had taken out the trash and had been for a moment out of sight at the back of the house.

"*No se ha muerto!*" Ricaurte wailed, kicking the tiles with his boots."*No se ha muerto!*" Tears tracked his dusty cheeks:" *No se ha muertoooo!*" Kiki looked scared too.

A balance had been restored, Carl thought. Yes, Ricaurte was acute; nothing in the world could have lifted him so high with Kiki but a Unimuck. But Kiki was just as acute. Real things, real things for Ricaurte were the mother in the kitchen who slept beside his cot, who bathed him in the aluminum tub on the back patio, set him to dry in the sun. Carl went back to the patio and sat, a little breathlessly, in the lounge chair. Linda was not around. She had missed it. Just as well.

AND THEN there was the matter of the increasingly bold actions of the press corps. How had Frank and Rainey lived so agreeably with them? Or maybe they hadn't. Maybe the death of their baby had not been the only reason for leaving. This matter came to a climax at the end of October, and it was the *Doña* who determined their next move.

Chapter 4

The fire must have started under the house. The wood floor burned through into the room Willi used for a studio. It was on the opposite end from the bedrooms, so they weren't alarmed until the whole side was in flames, and Elsie the dog barking wildly. Willi saved his short wave, a few of his paintings; and Augustina, her trunk from that side of the house. Blanche and Carl saved their clothes and Carl's books. Engines were summoned, and they stood out in the courtyard in front, the press corps dancing madly about, and watched it, all but the walls and grand staircase, burn to an empty shell. Miguelito had been parked across the street, so was saved.

Toward dawn they drove to the Pensión Stein on the Avenida Sexta and slept, the three of them, in one room, without washing their bodies or changing their smoky clothes; they didn't wake until three in the afternoon.

Willi was up first. Carl stirred.

"We can't stay here long you know," Willi said.

"No, no!" Carl sat up. Willi had washed and put on a pair of clean pants and a shirt he had rescued.

"All we need in one of those mud huts," Willi said. "We might build it ourselves, with help, or buy one; they can't cost much."

Carl thought about the thatched, whitewashed huts that ought to have been pretty, yet never were, due to a broken washing machine in the yard or the roof patched in piece of derelict tin or a crude sign painted up in raw aniline blue:

LIBERTAD PARA LOS PRISIONEROS DE VILLA PARDO.

He got dressed to go out.

"Where are you going?" Willi asked.

"To talk to the *Doña*.".

"OF COURSE, you must come to us at Tula," she told Carl, after he told her about the fire and Willi's idea of the mud hut. She sent him out to find *don* Rafa at the café.

Don Rafa was in his usual place at the Cafe Mil y Una Noches drinking *cafe tinto*. He ordered Carl a beer and a meat pie. Carl told him about the fire.

"How?"

"The press corps. I suspect. Kids who hang around us. They smoked in the *bodega*."

"You are all safe?"

"Yes, yes"

"Thank God! But the whole…"

"The whole grand pile. Left the granite staircase and a couple of walls."

"*Cielos!*"

"We need something. A shack. It must be cheap."

"Cheap, yes. A mud shack you mean, Una casa de behareque?"

"Yes. And a little land maybe."

"Mud shacks are in continual need of being shored up. That is if they don't wash away entirely in the rainy season, and *animalitos* infest the thatch aside from numerous other…"

"Your wife suggested Tula."

"Ah, you want to be farmers!"

"Willi would like it." He thought of all the agricultural advice from Fidel Castro that Willi had taken in over the short wave. Willi approved of agriculture.

"Yes, we could grow all our food."

"You will live like peasants."

"We are peasants." Willi loved peasants.

"Ah, well now, there is a concrete block hut with a good zinc roof at Las Brumas…

"Yes?"

"It has never been much of a farm. A vacation spot, belongs to my wife's family actually. I would have made it pay, but they never cared. There are two outbuildings, and one is empty. There was a caretaker, *don* Luciano, occupied it with his son. The son married and we built another for him. Then *don* Luciano moved up the hill to Los Franceses. The son does his work. There is little enough since we hardly go now. There was the accident. I fear *don*. Luciano blames himself. In any case, the house is empty. Plenty of land, plantains, bananas, some chickens, one cow for the milk.. There used to be pigs, horses. We used to go four or five months out of the year. All the long vacation with the children, the nephews."

"And why not now?"

"There was the accident. One of my brother's children was thrown from *don* Luciano's mule. That is he was dragged a good way from the stirrup and died of a broken neck. It was a sad occasion."

"Yes, God!"

"Though *doña* Berta has a deal of others to console herself with, I must say. My wife took it the hardest, had the mule and horses sold, and the pigs. We've turned to gardening. The margaritas thrive. Perhaps this year, the long vacation, we shall go again. But the hut you are welcome to."

"We would work."

"Ah, there is no need."

"We must work."

"But there is Orlando, and his woman helps in the kitchen."

"What is growing there now?"

"Margaritas, as I say. Bougainvillea."

"To eat, I mean."

"Well, there are plantains, and fodder. A cow was spared, did I say? There is a nearly empty stable. Your friend might do his painting there. Is he a good painter by the way?"

"He's a genius. Listen, we'll take your offer," Carl said. "But we must work."

"Work, then, *pues*, work," *don* Rafa smiled.

"CONCRETE BLOCK hut, zinc roof, plenty of land, in the central *cordillera* ..." Carl reported back. Blanche was still in bed, drinking iced coffee.

"We'll go!" Willi said, taking to the idea immediately as Carl had hoped. "We'll go immediately. Get dressed!" he told Blanche.

THEY GAVE ELSIE THE DOG to Augustina, and the Renault to Ramos to sell for them; it would never make it over the *cordillera*. The Laundry Magnate made a few feeble gestures at blaming them for the fire, but gave it up in the face of their poverty and the testimony of the baker next door that the urchins continually smoked under the house.

At the Casa del Pueblo they outfitted themselves as cheaply as possible with new clothes; and the following Thursday they took a bus to the city to catch a *por puesto* taxi to Tuxpan in the state of Tula.

Carl, Willi, and Blanche

II. State of Tula

Carl, Willi, and Blanche

Chapter 1

The terminal was off the Paseo San Martin in the Capital. They paid their fare inside and registered with the police at the control stall. You couldn't cross a state line without doing this. Carl bought a copy of "Bohemia": Eduardo Mompos, *El Rey del Merengue* on the cover.

The terminal was large and modern, but filthy and crowded, so they waited outside for a driver to make up the five fares to Tuxpan. The city was hot and dry at noon, and smelled of ozone. Drivers crowded around: "Two more for Oichichinango, leaving immediately. "Tequello, this.'way. "One more for Tequello over here." A drunken soldier offered Blanche the last place in his taxi. She pointed to their waiting driver.

"Never mind; you go right now with us."

She looked away and he shuffled on. Their fourth passenger, a bewildered old woman in black, watched the driver stow a large untidy bundle in the trunk. A string bag wrapped around a crumpled paper bag she kept to herself. A legless man strapped to a platform mounted on rollerskates conversed with waiting drivers. Finally a last fare was secured, a salesman with a display case and a large moustache.

The protocol of *por puesto* riders was the first three fares had window seats, but the old woman confused matters by letting Blanche in the front first then taking the prime front window. Their driver wouldn't allow this, ordered them all out and rearranged. "Too fat," grumbled, the old woman, shifting her string bag. Carl and Will had the back windows, the salesman in between. "Too fat, too fat," Blanche was unable to close the front door; the driver leaned across and pulled it to. "Listen, old one, are you sure you know where you're going?" The woman searched her bag for an address, which she found on a dirty slip of paper she passed to the driver. He took it brusquely, nodded, and pulled out to deal swiftly and surely with the city traffic.

In a matter of seconds they were soaring along the aerial ribbon that crossed the city, leaving to its own slow pace the fussy old town below, its cafes and verandahs behind bougainvillea vines. Autopista del Este, Autopista del Valle; then, looping westward, onto an older mountain road.

They climbed into the clouds hanging over the city. Carl opened "Bohemia" which revealed Eduardo Mompos leading a double life: a certain four year old living in a shack on the Ávila with his mother, an employee in a shirt factory, held indisputably to be son of the singer, recently wed to a starlet. The air grew cooler, thinner. The salesman and the driver discussed the *Cinco y Seis*::"Twice he won 80,000 pesos with five horses. I sat up half the night with my brother-in-law filling out the *bendita* form. He wanted Radiodifusora in the sixth. I kept telling him don't put the favorite. He would not listen to me, and it turned out if he'd put Samaranta he'd have won. Twenty-eight winners splitting 15 million pesos! I meant to help him, knowing how his pension is nothing after the devaluation ."

They crossed a nearly dried up river. A cyclist in a ragged bathing suit washed his clothes, stretching them on a rock to bleach. The road was a raw, red gash in the mountainside; below them were the red and green Eternit roofs of the weekend houses. On the opposite slope was a Polar Beer sign lettered in white stones; *Gomas* Goodyear, lettered in white painted tires.

A bank of clouds sat on the blue eucalyptus treetops. A shower hung over the far valley. Suddenly the clouds opened and they overlooked the city. They passed two vans, tarps flapping. The driver switched on a daytime drama: Little life-wearied laundress, support of eight fatherless…

They crossed a second river, then climbed again, the gash this time on their right. A small metal cross with a hubcap hanging on it marked the spot where a car had gone over the cliff. The little laundress breathed her last, became an angel in heaven, guided her Alfonso's steps into manhood. The woman in front offered guava pastries. Willi accepted one. Blanche felt sick.

"There's San Antonio below," the driver pointed it out, lovely village of white washed houses with heavy black thatch. A square with a church. Grass bleached colorless.

HEXAMINE: PURGE LIVER AND GUT

Written on a wall. A woman milled corn on a doorstep. The road wound up. Hollywood, La Florida. In La Florida storekeepers threw pails of water on the street to keep down the dust. The market stalls were closing. Mangos, papayas rotted in the sun. From the *cantina* came the voice of Eduardo Mompos:" En un Playon de Putomayo." A wooden bodied bus was off the road with a blowout. A woman with a chicken on a lease waited. The way was so narrow here that houses were flush with the road.

LIBERTY FOR THE PRISQNERS OF EL CONDOR.

Painted on a wall. As they neared the snowcap, only dusty *penca* weed grew, and a few paddle cactus. A lizard twitched, held immobile, staring.

Then down, to Bermeja. Here they stopped at a *relleno* emporium. A large, cement block structure with an open front strung with clotheslines on which were hung *chorizos*, red peppers, inflatable plastic toys, *fotonovelas*, transistor radios, paperback manuals on hypnosis, plaster of Paris saints. At the back was a stainless steel counter where they made the *rellenos*, bins of apples and melons. They bought white cheese and a couple expensive apples.

Buses and *por puesto* taxis pulled in and out. Blanche went to the bathroom; Carl and Willi sat on a children's swing set and ate. The waxy red apples, imported from Washington State, were cottony and brown inside. "Enough nostalgia," Willi said.

Their driver collected them. They descended in a broad arc, stopping at a guard post where a guard checked police registration numbers, and entered a narrow, parched valley.

Only the irrigated cane fields were green here. Houses and trees were dusty and diminutive except for the *hacendado's* houses marked by stately crossings of tall palms. The surrounding hills were burning here and there, the smoke adding to the heat and dust.

Too many rocky slopes stood now between them and the capital radio station, which was replaced by a powerful new valley voice: sorrows of another laundress's son who cannot marry his Merceditas because his taxi has been stolen.

At La Encrucijada the salesman got out. They circled a plaza full of fruit vendors and returned to the highway. Driving into Tuxpan, smoke rolled across the highway from a field of burning cane stumps. They closed the windows, suffocated. The old woman wanted out in a *barrio* of rutted roads on the outskirts of town. They lurched around a little square. "Son of a bitch pot holes in this town," rumbled the driver.

"Right here is fine," said the old woman.

The final stop was a taxi stand in front of the cathedral. They got out and unloaded their duffel bags from the roof. It was near dusk; and since there was no electricity at Las Brumas and *don* Rafa advised not arriving at night, they went across the street and reserved two rooms at a dim little hotel with tall spindly wooden pillars holding up an arcade around a patio full of rubber plants and paddle cactus.

Tuxpan was a town of maybe three streets of commerce and apartment houses, intersected by two broad boulevards. They walked along one of these boulevards, which was lined with large houses set behind high walls, and found a Chinese restaurant, Chinese restaurants here were identical to Chinese restaurants in Chicago, or presumably anywhere. This one was consoling in their homeless state. They ordered shrimp, chicken, and pork. Will took out the account book and wrote figures on a napkin: They had about two thousand pesos saved plus eight hundred for the Renault. "It's my opinion," Willi said, "we should spend only on items like clothes, dentists and food we can't grow, like meat, or we could give up meat."

"We could."

"There will be eggs and milk."

"We can grow beans, yucca, plantains. We'll each have our jobs: cooking, washing up, washing clothes, plus the cows…"

"Cow," Carl said.

"Yes, and the chickens."

"Have you ever had dealings with chickens?"

"Never. We'll learn. There's a caretaker, *don* Luciano's son, who's also night watchman. We'll watch him. You know," Willi said, "People live here for three pesos a day. The price of a Coke in a hotel."

"Who told you that?"

"Augustina. I was taking instruction from Augustina. In *la pobreza*. You can live a week on a pound of dried beans, a couple pounds of yucca and rice, a cake of raw sugar, some plantains: That's eight pesos a week in the city, less in the country.

"What else do you need? A couple pair of cutoffs; you wash them in a stream now and then; dental care, you can't neglect that; the poor don't bother, I know, but I don't agree with that. A bicycle; that's a legitimate expense. We'll get one, use buses for the rest. Reduce things. You need a philosophy of things. What's dispensable, what's not…What was I saying? Oh, fluoride treatments, indispensable. Underwear, dispensable. Socks, I admit, have their function, unless you can dispense with shoes. Sandals, an excellent invention. Shaving, a waste of time, especially if you use dispensable blades. Running to the store for dispensable items is dispensable.…"

"Go fuck yourself Willi. I'll shave my frigging legs if I feel like it," Blanche said.

NEXT DAY they bought tequila, rice, lentils, beans, salt, soap, kerosene, matches, seeds, candles, and took a bus up the mountain just before noon.

Kilómetro Veinticinco was a collection of three or four houses, a small store with a telephone exchange behind. Las Brumas was up the road about a half mile, overlooking the small settlement. They hiked up the hill with backpacks and bedrolls. Several mud huts crowded against the road, sunbaked and crazed like old china. Children in earth colored rags played in the doorways. The road doubled back and Las Brumas came into sight, a wooden house painted white, with a red Eternit roof. The hillside was planted with coffee bushes shaded by plantain trees. Behind the house a pasture sloped steeply up. At the top was a cistern covered with a large concrete slab, and behind that another farmhouse.

Breathless, they stopped to rest. Leaning against the ferrous red gash where the road was carved into the mountainside, they put down the packs and gulped the thin air.

Another turn, and the drive up to the house ran off to the right. The house was surrounded by a garden with gravel paths. There were beds of begonia, marguerites, gardenia, limoncillo. The *Doña's* work, Carl thought. The two huts were at the back in a plantain grove off a dirt courtyard. They were substantial, concrete block structures with zinc roofs. In the doorway of the smaller one a girl stood watching them. Orlando's wife. She was awkwardly built with a large head, probably looked older than she was.

"*Buenas,*" Carl said, and asked for Orlando.

"*Arriba,*" she said, pointing up the slope.

Followed by her stare, they looked around. Opposite the huts was a stable with four stalls and a gleaming forage cutter. Coffee beans were spread to dry on the roof and a bougainvillea vine covered the sides. A wash was hung to dry over the vines; another soaked in a bucket:

Their hut, which had been used by Orlando's father until his wife died, was furnished with a wood stove, some pots and pans and dishes, two beds with horsehair mattresses, and an old mahogany wardrobe. On the small front porch were a metal table and chairs and a small wooden bench painted blue.

"Excellent, excellent," Willi 'kept saying. "Nothing but what's necessary." They put away the groceries on two shelves over the stove and unrolled the bedrolls on the two beds. Willi took the back room and Carl and Blanche took the room off the kitchen. Willi started a fire in the stove with some kindling piled on the floor, but found this made the hut unbearably hot. He noticed that the girl had started to cook outside over a small kerosene stove; so, enduring her stares, he fabricated a barbecue with three cement blocks he found around back, and the grill out of the wood stove's oven rack.

Carl walked up the hill and found Orlando coming down with the red cow and a black dog with a pig's tail. He was tall, curly-haired, *mestizo*. "But the *Doña* isn't here," he kept saying, unable to imagine that any gringo would be visiting in the absence of *doña* Luz.

"To help with the work," Carl explained; but this idea seemed unacceptable to Orlando.

"I do the work. Where you from?" he said suddenly in English.

"Chicago."

"I live there," Orlando said.

"Where?"

"Texas, California. I dream all the time to go back."

Carl laughed.

"Why you come here? There is nothing here."

"Our house we were renting in Las Marias burned. The *Doña* offered us, the hut, Luciano's hut. We want to work, you show us…."

"Show you?"

"Yes."

Orlando simply stared at Carl." OK, OK. You hiding out from something?"

"Sort of."

"Ah," This, Orlando understood. The cow was pushed into the stable. "I milk her now."

Will left the fire and followed them in." This is Willi." Carl said.

"Hiya." Orlando took an aluminum pan from a nail and began filling it." You can't go back there?"

"We can go back," Willi said." If we want to."

"You take me?"

"We plan to live here."

"Nobody lives here. What you do, you have to leave?"

"I thought you milked cows in the morning." Willi said.

"Morning and afternoon." He handed Willi the pan filled with milk. "Take. We don't drink."

Blanche came in. She had washed her hair under the spigot, and put on shorts. Orlando stared at her and she gave him a frank look. Then he laughed.

Carl inspected the forage cutter's circular blade, oiled and gleaming. Under it was a bin of *caña brava* minced fine. He touched an old saddle hung in the corner.

"Used to be a horse," Orlando said. One of the *Doña's* nephews fell off and broke his neck." His eyes kept going to Blanche.

"This is Blanche," Carl said.

"Your woman or his?"

"Mine."

Orlando handed the second pan of milk to Carl.

"No, you should have one of them."

"I tell you we don't drink. I was a maintenance man in Texas for some Christian Science people. I take care of 'a cooling plant. I do painting, repairing. All those things. They take care of me, but they don't like me drink, smoke. They interfere with my life."

"Your wife should drink milk," Will said. The girl was pregnant. She stood in the doorway staring at them. Very young; fourteen or fifteen. "When is the baby?"

"January."

There wasn't enough firewood to finish the lentils. Willi moved them to Orlando's stove. They shared some fried plantains and sat around the oil lamp at the metal table drinking Cruz Verde. We'll get a kerosene stove when we go down to Tuxpan next," Willi said. "And a pressure cooker." He was exhausted from his outdoor fire.

The darkness around them was filled with *cigarras* trilling and the mists had begun to descend. The girl, whose name was Miriam, washed up her pans at the spigot in the yard, using the red dust as an abrasive. No one had heard her speak beyond that first word.

"The *Doña* make us marry," Orlando said sheepishly, looking at her.

"A pressure cooker," Willi said. "Cultivating fork, cheese cloth, a colander, garden hose, sprinkler. I'll try bush beans behind the stable there, and transplant some of that yucca growing wild. Have you had any luck with corn?" he asked Orlando.

"Not much. No rains till December."

"That's what the hose is for?"

"We run water down for few days. Now is dried up."

"No, man, I've looked at that cistern," said Willi. It only needs cleaning.

He was trying to get Fidel on the short wave saved from the fire; but succeeded only in pulling in a powerful Bonair gospel station.

THE NIGHT WAS COLD and damp as the clouds came down. Carl got up twice to close the shutters and to throw the wool ponchos over them. Toward dawn he fell deeply asleep and woke late to the stove going, dispelling the damp and brewing coffee. Carl got up, wrapping himself in a poncho.

The clouds had begun to rise, though some remained caught in the bluish eucalyptus trees of the lower slopes; patches of weak sunlight filtered through. He stood out on the porch and watched Orlando come down from the boundary of the *Doña's* land. Carl brought him coffee and together they pulled the steaming cow out of the stall. Orlando milked her and put her into the near pasture. They minced forage; what they had cut the night before was nearly gone. Carl went behind the stable to where the cane grew and cut down stalks with a machete, while Orlando put them through the hand-operated cutter. When Carl had filled the bin with stalks, he watched Orlando, then took a turn himself at the revolving blade, working until his arms ached.

Orlando went to bed then, after his night of patrolling the boundaries, and the girl, Miriam, came out to resume her silent washing by the pump in the yard.

Willi fried plantains and heated the milk for the coffee; then they walked down to the store below to buy bundles of firewood. The day was warming up and they sat at a wooden table in front of the little store drinking rum in chunky glasses. The storekeeper's wife had left for the.market in Tuxpan before dawn and was back with a side of fatback, a beef heart, some soup bones, a basketful of tomatoes and cucumbers, and a string bag full of *aracacha* root. These she would retail to the poor shack dwellers around. She agreed to bring them a kerosene stove on her next trip, and sold them some bones and a couple tomatoes.

"We won't come here often," Willi said, but Carl had a feeling they would.

Carl, Willi, and Blanche

They spent the rest of the morning transplanting the young yucca plants that had gone wild into a plot beside the stable. For lunch they had more fried plantains and a salad made from The *Doña's* lettuce and the tomatoes. Carl fell asleep after, woke to the smell of Willi's *ocote* fire in the courtyard, bitter in his nostrils. Miriam was cooking too, over the petroleum stove on the porch. He had never been so aware of these processes of food gathering, preparation, and eating.

The late afternoon sun was warm, the air dry and clear. He wandered about the grounds, through vegetable gardens overgrown with *caña brava* and purple castor, swept and empty stables, plantain grove beside it, then a lean-to chicken house with shelves for roosting, fenced-in yard for scratching. There were some white leghorns with two or three baby chicks, a scrawny rooster. A leather-covered account book hung from a chain. Twenty-four leghorns, purchased Feb. 9, noted on the flyleaf. Inside were twenty-four columns with daily checks or zeros posted. Most of them seemed to lay daily at the beginning, less now. How was it kept straight? Behind the hen house he found an aluminum wire cage with twenty-four compartments, twelve each side. He went back and counted the chickens: seventeen; one or two looked ill.

"Leghorns," Orlando said behind him. "Don't lay much anymore, and no good to eat; *muy flacos.*" They collected the eggs. Only six. "Not much good for nothing, *estas criaturas,*" Orlando said. He scattered some corn. Carl moved on, through the plantain grove to the side of the big house which overlooked the valley.

The *Doña's* flowers were planted in neat rectangular beds outlined with white painted stones, pebble paths between. *Margaritas*, gardenias, *veranera*, *inmortales*, he recognized; most he couldn't name. One should know the names of things, he thought. When she came he would ask her, note the names in his notebook. Would she come? He felt her presence in these well-weeded and watered rectangles, these neat paths.

There was a glassed-in porch on this side of the house, with cement steps painted red. He went up and looked through the panes. There were some blocky red leatherette chairs at one end, a table covered in blue oilcloth with eight odd chairs around, a bookcase with some games: Chinese checkers, a few creamy paperbacks of the kind the *Doña* sent out to be bound in leather. The door was unlocked so he went in. He checked a few of the books to see, from the cut and uncut pages, where she had read. The French novels were mostly cut open; of the English titles she had read in their entirety only some essays of David Grayson and Lin Yutang. He had never heard of either..

He continued around the house. There were rosebushes trained against the wall, a fig tree in green fruit, a bed of herbs: *manzanilla, culantro,* false *azafran,* a *limoncillo* bush. She had served him an infusion once made with *limoncillo* leaves. He picked a leaf and put it in his pocket, then continued around the house looking in windows: a room containing two double decker bunks, the kitchen, a large room with wire-screened cabinets and a red tile floor, a wooden chair painted blue before an oilcloth covered table. She will come, he thought.

The woman from the little store brought them back a kerosene stove next day which greatly simplified cooking and allowed it to be done indoors. After that Carl did the errands. He went to the market on the early bus, arriving before seven. At one stall he bought rice, lentils, black beans; at another, tomatoes, corn, cucumbers, which were their staples. Then, leaving his basket in the care of a lottery seller, he went to a cafe across the street from the main entrance to the market and had two small cups of *tinto* and a *mil hojas* pastry, and read one of the books from the *Doña's* library. Afterwards, wandering along Calle Tres de Mayo he occasionally bought an enamel bowl or a set of pottery cups.

"But why do you buy these things?" Blanche complained, "weighing us down."

"What do you mean?"

"Well it isn't as if we'd meant to come just here. To Kilometro Veinticinco," she said.

"Where, then?" he asked.

"I don't know. I don't know."

IN NOVEMBER, they had their own lettuce, beans, and some yucca. The figs were ripe and Willi put them up in a syrup of agua panela. He learned to make white cheese from the left over milk, letting it stand three days, then pouring off the whey through a cloth and salting it heavily.

Carl brought back a new white rooster from the market, leading it on a leash. The hens were allowed to roost and six little leghorns were hatched. These, when they were big enough, were placed in the cages, over which Carl improvised a roof out of some pieces of Eternit scattered behind the stable. Two died inexplicably, but he bought eight more and filled one-half of the cage. These last were reds which made nice broilers once they were done laying, Orlando said. The cages had to be cleaned daily and the water troughs kept carefully filled, the roof cooled down with pails of water in the noon heat. Carl numbered them and noted their existence in a fresh page of the notebook hanging from the wall. He tried giving each a name, but they were indifferent creatures.

"I mean it isn't as if we meant to come exactly here," Blanche said from the bed, watching Carl hang up a weaving bought from an Indian claimed to have walked here from La Virginia. A monkey with a triangular green face and a tree. "The monkey is bigger than the tree," said Blanche. Crazy." She was drinking *agave* tea.

"The monkey is closer," said Carl." Or more important, that's more likely. Yes, that's it." He looked at her. "Where is it you want to go then?" he asked.

"How do I know, if we just sit here on this mountain."

Carl sat down on the bed. "You oughtn't to drink that stuff."

"It does no harm. Only the *mescal* harms. It makes me feel good, bigger than this mountain. I'm like that monkey, bigger than the tree, bigger than the mountain. If only we hadn't sold the car, Carl, Carl."

"You want to stay with me?"

"No... yes."

"You'd have left me if we were back there?"

"Maybe, maybe not."

"You're free. We said we'd be free."

"Oh, Carl, Carl."

"What do you want? What?"

"Hold me. I'm big. I'm bigger than this mountain."

"You shouldn't...."

"Hold me!" She was naked, perspiring. They rocked together. "I want..."

"What? What?"

"I want Belle."

"You can't stand her."

"Help me, Carl, help me. I'm disappearing." They lay together, perspiring.

"Did you do it with Lennie McWhirter?" she whispered.

"Never."

"What did you do with her?"

"Talk."

"And the *Doña?*"

"The *Doña!*"

"What did you talk about with her?"

"Churches."

"Churches. Oh, hold me hold me, don't move...Yes, yes, it's a nice monkey. His face is green and his tail zigzags. His face is green and he's bigger than the tree, ha ha. Tell me, tell me about churches. What church do you talk about?"

"Chartres. It has two towers. Built in different centuries. The older one is finer."

"Why?"

"It solves the problem of changing from a square to a hexagon ."

"Ah, hexagon...Don't move, don't move. Is that what the *Doña* worries about? Changing from a square to a...?"

"She's a good woman."

"Am I good?"

"Yes. I wish you could be happy."

"I'm hot."

"Just lie quiet."

"I can't, Carl; that's what I'm trying to tell you."

"Why, why?"

"It's death. I feel death here."

"What death?"

"That child."

"What child?"

"That fell from the horse. I don't know, the hens. Willi's beans. Death, Carl."

"I don't understand. An accident. A couple hens..."

"It's here. It's why they don't come."

"They'll come."

"No. Hold me, hold me. The bed's floating."

"You shouldn't..."

"Hold me, come in me. But don't move. Come in me and stay still, so I'll stay on earth."

They lay together, bathed in sweat.

"How am I good, Carl?"

"You came with me. You're mine."

"Oh, Carl."

"What? What?"

"If I was back there, I'd go. I'd stick out my thumb and go. Here I can't; I can't even talk the stupid language."

"Try, try to learn. Talk to Miriam."

"Miriam doesn't talk. She stares. I can't bear it. I can't stay put, Carl. Since I was sixteen, I can't stay put…churches. Your old lady talks about churches. That's funny. She's old, Carl…"

"Not so old. Younger than him."

"Forty at least. She can't have children."

"She's good, good."

"How, good, how?"

"…takes care of us all. Orlando, Miriam, the gardens, the nephews, us."

"Old, Carl. That's what I feel about them. They're old. Hundreds, thousands of years older than we are. Don't you feel it?"

"Maybe."

"You like it. You like to read her old books. But you don't see. It's death."

"She brings up her brother's children. They have nothing. She sends them to good schools."

"And *don* Rafa brings up the children of the *telegrafista*."

"Who says that."

"Everyone knows they're his." She held out the cup to him. "Drink."

"No."

"It's very mild."

He sipped the musty tasting infusion. Felt nothing. Like Willi, he preferred Cruz Verde Rum.

"Death, Carl, it's death I feel in my bones. Fuck me, fuck me now, yes…!"

EACH DAY WAS SUNNY as the previous one. It was the *verano*. The pastures were brown, and above *Los Franceses*, fires blackened the mountain. One of Carl's young reds died, and three more of the old Leghorns.

Chapter 2

At the end of November the big house was opened up. The daughter of the *Telegrafista* came up to cook and Orlando's wife moved over to help in the kitchen. A week later the *Doña* arrived with *doña* Bertha and the four nephews, who slept in the bunk beds in the annex to the house beside the garage. They would stay through Christmas, the *Doña*, perhaps longer.

Three large meals were prepared daily. Occasionally, when the kitchen in the big house became too hot, dishes were baked in Orlando's oven and carried over to the house. Sometimes, the remains of a meal, a *flan*, or a dish of baked plantains with white cheese would be sent out to them afterward.

THE DOÑA'S ENGLISH LESSONS resumed at ten every morning. They met on the glass-enclosed porch at the back of the house overlooking the garden with the gravel paths.

"Have you everything you need?" she asked him in her careful English on the first day.

"Oh, yes. The woman at the *abasto* brings us supplies from Tuxpan, and I go once a week."

"You must go with Juan while we are here."

"Thank you."

"They charge too much, at the *abasto*. I know you have limited...and I wish to pay you the hundred pesos weekly for the lessons."

"But it is too much," he said, "We are living here without paying."

"No, no, I wish to pay. Also, there is my nephew. He may also receive the lesson. He has brought his book from school."

"You are very kind."

Orlando's woman brought a tray with *café tinto* and some white rolls. She stared at Carl, unable to comprehend that someone who cleaned out the hen house was also received here in the big house and served by herself.

"The little boys come here to recover their health on the vacation. The air of the mountains opens the appetite. We do not have, how do you call... the change of season, so the body suffers unless one changes the altitude."

"It is very beautiful here."

"Yes, when it suns."

"When the sun shines," he corrected her.

"When the sun shines as now there is nowhere more beautiful. When it rains it is a sad climate some say."

"And you?"

"It is my home. My family is of Tuxpan. It is pleasing to me, the high, the cold, the black pines, the white houses…."

He watched her face. It was pale as usual, but animated. She had been wearing black since she arrived. It seemed that a cousin had died, and the women in the family had adopted *luto*. The black had shocked him when she first arrived, and made her look haggard, but today she had thrown a blue sweater over her shoulders and was wearing a pair of slacks for the country. It was believed that one should spend a part of each year in the mountains to benefit one's health, she had told him. He could see today that it benefited hers.

He told her she looked well.

"The place where one is from, where one has been happy," she said. "It is a climate for serious men they say. My grandfather wore always a black hat and a cloak. He could recite all of Robledo by heart."

"And why did you leave?"

"I marry. *Don* Rafa dislikes here. He has arguments with the priests at the seminary where they sent him." She laughed. "One day he put his desk on his head—at the seminary you must buy everything, books, desk, everything—he put his desk on his head one day and left there and would never go back…

"But it must bore you;" she turned her fine eyes on him, "a woman's life."

"No, no, why ever?" he cried, embarrassing her.

"The cow does well," she said, turning the subject.

"Yes, yes."

"She is old, but she does well, yes; when we are living in the city, drinking the milk from the store that one never knows what they put in it, I say to *don* Rafa, 'What a grateful thing it is to come here and drink the milk of a cow that is…how do you say, *una vaca conocida?*'"

"A cow one is acquainted with."

"Yes, yes," she laughed. A cow one is acquainted with." She looked him timidly in the face. "You will go back to your country one day, I am sure."

"No, no, never to that."

"That what?"

"That waiting to begin. Nothing could begin."

"But one's county!" she said.

"One's county…one's county drops bombs where there is nothing to bomb. Everyone knows it is a disgrace, and yet it has gone so far it cannot be stopped, or anyone say it's been for nothing. Not now."

"Still, it will be over one day. You will go back."

"I cannot for now, in any case."

"I cannot understand it," she said. "To have such a dislike for one's country. We criticize ourselves all the time, as you notice…my husband. Yet we never do not love."

Carl was thoughtful. "You know what I did once. I stole the bust of my great grandfather that stood in the lobby of the administration building of the college, and hid it in my closet."

"How is that?"

"It was a week of…initiation for the new class. The college was founded by my great grandfather, so I had a scholarship. The whole thing embarrassed me. It was a tradition for one of the freshmen to steal it every year. So that year I was chosen. It cost me a lot of money because I didn't have anyone to help me and I couldn't lift the thing myself. I hired a trucking firm in town to bring it to me at night and hide it in my closet. I hated the whole thing, I hated that whole year. It was the most awful thing to know he was in my closet. I couldn't even think about it."

"So he was a famous man then?"

"In a very small way. A clergyman who went west to start churches and colleges. One of my aunts wrote a very depressing book about him. He just went back and forth between Connecticut and Nebraska on horseback, enormous journeys. She said he kept journals of the birds and plants he came across, but no one could find the journals. And then it was just that

I was *expected* to go to that college and take the required Old Testament course, and sit in daily chapel and steal that bust…

"And all those journeys. What did they mean to him? My father was a traveler. Only he sold encyclopedias and textbooks. He took me with him once. We stayed in these awful motels. It was so lonely. And my mother was so lonely. No one could bear it and nothing was ever explained and one day he didn't come home anymore. He took up drinking and all my uncles took up drinking and that was the present-day Brown family: travelers and drunks and failures. So what did any of it mean?

"But the college wasn't so bad. There was the really good organ. There was Bach, you know, and literature. There was this professor who first gave me Henry Adams to read…"

"Yes, yes," she said thoughtfully. One of her small nephews had come into the room and was sitting under the desk playing with a toy car. "Will you have a cookie, my child?" she asked him.

He nodded.

"Come, then." She held out one of the little cakes, which he came to take from her, leaning against her knees as he ate it, his face shyly averted from Carl who caused his aunt to talk so strangely.

"I am afraid it is a custom here," she said, caressing the child, "for sons of wealthy families to buy…how shall I say? To pay a sum to avoid the conscription."

"I could have done that," Carl said. "That is I could have stayed…in school; but I'm glad I didn't. It is better, as Willi says, to reject, to make one's life a statement."

"I do not understand, I'm afraid," she said. The child leaned heavily against her, pressing for her attention. "How can one reject one's entire… that is to say…one's life?"

"I had a cousin," Carl said. "We lived fifteen years in adjoining houses. He wanted to go to fight; he needed to bloody someone, to get bloodied. I felt it too, till Willi. In any case, he's dead, my cousin."

"Ah…"

"He was over there seventy-eight hours. Is it possible in seventy-eight hours to get gloriously bloodied, I wonder? I don't know what he imagined it would be like."

"I have no son …" she said.

"Do you despise me?" he interrupted.

"Despise you? But hardly know you," she said, innocent of how she injured him.

Doña Berta, the mother of the boy, came in and called him to her. "He is no trouble," said *doña* Luz, allowing the child to slip from her lap. *Doña* Berta, who had eight children, was a small woman with a narrow dark face. She was married to a brother of *don* Rafa's who was relatively poor. At eleven every morning she played hearts on the verandah with *misia* Eulalia and her daughter from up the hill.

"I don't know," Carl said. "I can't explain it, but my first *positive* feeling in these past four or five years has been deciding to come here…" He felt slightly off balance, having been interrupted by the child's mother as he was about to tell her more of it, the waiting, the impossibility of beginning a life when everything depended on a draft number, but, as she had said, she barely knew him.

One of the other nephews was shouting below in the garden. She got up and called the little boy to her: "My child, you are all in a perspiration."

"But," she said to Carl," You have ruin your career, your life. What is there for you here?"

"This place. Useful work."

"I'm afraid it is not a…how you say…a serious farm. The soil is poor, the hens. It is for the air we come, the flowers…" She moved a gray porcelain dove to a high shelf out of reach of the child. "Still, your mother, she is sad. It is such a distance. I mean, to live in a foreign country."

"You learn a foreign language," he said.

"Ah, but it is only to travel as a tourist, to read, perhaps. You think it is useless, that I should rather play hearts with the others?"

"No, no! I admire you. You are altogether admirable!"

"An idle woman."

"No, you must read! And you might travel; but you said you never would again."

"Never as I once did."

"How is that?"

"Young. Alone." She laughed.

"What is funny?"

"It is an old family joke. An old aunt, very rich, she never left Envigado. They had a farm there, a very old-fashioned family. One year her husband made great preparations, took a train at La Victoria and a ship at Los Olmos, and went to Europe. My aunt stayed in Envigado and crocheted her tablecloths and played games of *tute* and drank her chocolate at eleven. She sighed when she thought of her husband. 'The poor man. Alone in Paris,' she would say."

"Ah, yes, yes!" he laughed. How charming she was when she told these stories..

"Alone in Paris, ah yes. Will you have a biscuit?"

"Thank you."

"It is a terrible thing, the bombing. You are not mistaken I hope," she said.

"It is to be heard every evening on the radio."

"Ah, then I suppose it must be true, the radio." She turned her gray eyes on him. Charming woman. What had produced her? What slow education, what long breeding produced these reticences, these occasional drolleries, this deep gaze? "But shall we go on?" she said.

"Yes, we shall go on."

CARL TOOK OVER some of the care of the Cow One Knows. He ran sheaves of tough *casa brava* through the foliage cutter and heaped it into her trough. One day while he was in there he found a book of poems, Alejandro Páez, *Una Vaina de Palabras*, on a sill in the stable where *don* Rafa had stored some old notebooks. The notebooks were spotted with mold from the moisture of the clouds that enveloped the farm until about ten o'clock every morning, and the book, printed in Mexico on the thick creamy paper of most of the *Doña's* books but not bound, had picked up a bit of the mold. He took it to the ragged hammock he had hung among the coffee bushes behind the stable and read one of the longish poems toward the end. It was called "The Place Where Judas Lost His Boots". It turned out to be a voice he could follow, human, bitter, groping. The derisive voice of *don* Rafa, but caught up in a kind of helpless love of these mountains, over which the poems led him to believe the poet was making a foot journey. He read to the end and then started at the beginning. Here and there in the margins, someone, probably *don* Rafa, had written phrases and words in English, probably attempting a translation..

BLANCHE WASHED the way Miriam did, soaping the clothes with a green naphtha bar and spreading them on the grassy verge of the courtyard in the sun to bleach; then holding them under the spigot and stretching them over the *veranera* vines to dry. They often washed together, but the girl never spoke. Blanche had never heard her utter more than two syllables together, even to Orlando. If I had a child in me I'd be the same, like a bitch in the sun, Blanche thought.

After the washing the clothes, she washed her hair and shaved her legs. Carl brought her blades despite Willi's desire to let all hair grow. She let her armpits sprout, but not her legs. Then, with a sprig of *veranera*, she cleaned under her toenails, between her teeth, into her ears, around her clitoris, sniffing herself with pleasure. A dun-colored iguana watched her. She was hidden from curious eyes by the *veranera*, but she didn't care who looked at her. If John had been with her she'd have given him a sniff. He liked to smell her, she remembered, when she went without a bath in the days she was moving from place to places, staying wherever she could.

The burning *ocote* reminded her of autumn. She thought of Belle putting gourds in a bowl. Here it was summer, *verano*, but only some weather the wind brought over the *cordillera*. And there was no autumn.

Nearby, Willi worked dung into the soil and set out his tomato and pepper seedlings. The seeds Luciano gave him had begun to sprout: Amaranth, ancient food of the Aztecs. He planned to upgrade the fodder with it, use leaves and beans in soup. It was a nearly forgotten food according to Luciano. Willi had written his father to research it.

He noted the rain clouds hung over the *cordillera*. Let them come soon, he thought, sprinkling the seedlings as much as he dared. The cistern was low. Just past noon. He used the new shit hole behind the plantains, covered his contribution to the collection of night soil with loose clay. It was preferable to the latrine, in being less smelly. After, he took a shower in the stall behind the stable, washing his cutoffs and his T-shirt at the same time. The red clay stains didn't come out completely. He hung the clothes over the wall of the shower stall to dry and pulled on a clean shirt and a clean pair of cutoffs hanging there. They were stiff and scratchy and the pockets had fallen off, but serviceable. He passed Blanche, behind the *veranera*, smoking. She handed him her little clay pipe. It was rather good stuff, bought in the Café Media Luna from an old *marijuanero*. Marijuana until recently was an old man's drug here, as was *mescal*.

"You never draw me anymore."

"I'll draw you now." He went to the hut for his pad.

"Shall I take off my things?"

"No."

"Why? I always used to in Las Marias."

"All right. May as well get all the joints and muscles."

She stepped out of her shorts and pulled off her jersey. "Is that all you get?"

"Frankly, no."

"Is that true, Willi?"

"I feel like any other man."

"Then why don't you want me?"

"I control myself."

"Why bother?"

"Like Gandhi, I use the energy for other things."

"Did he draw naked women?"

"He took young women in his bed and never touched them."

"Stuff!"

"Truth."

"How do you want me?"

"Bend your left knee and raise yourself on your elbow."

"What if they touched him?"

"Who?"

"Gandhi. What if the women touched him?"

"He didn't say. Put your arm across your belly."

"Like this?"

"Yeah. Relax it more; spread your fingers like you had them."

CARL AND THE DOÑA walked among the *margaritas*, sat under the fig tree. She had adopted *semiluto* for the country, which meant she wore the black slacks with a figured blouse. She alternated between one with black dots and another with a faint purple flower pattern. She carried today two gardenias in her right hand. Like the Virgin, he thought, who carried lilies, or rather a scepter entwined with lilies as a sign of her power; and in the left hand an ermine as a sign of her support among the nobles, according to Henry Adams.

"How I have missed this, here," she said. "We have not come for over two years. One of my nephews…"

"I know," Carl said. "Orlando told us.

"He was thirteen. As a young child he was often ill. He had asthma and he was overweight. We had to have his teeth straightened." She began pulling the dead blossoms off of the bush, throwing them into a pile of compost. *Flores marchitas.*

"But he had the most loving nature. We thought he would go through life like that: a little lazy, without many friends. His mother liked him least of her children, I'm afraid, but he was my favorite. Always he came to me with his troubles.

"'I'm going to be a better student,' he said to me one day, and began to bring me his lessons." She sat on a bench at the end of the garden, where you could overlook the *abasto*. Then he lost his weight. The braces came off; the illnesses were less frequent; he exercised more; became more like other children."

She fingered the blooms in her lap. The youngest nephew came out of the house and ran into the garden.

"He was beginning life. A beautiful boy. 'I'll be an engineer like *tio* Rafa,' he'd say.

"Ah, well; it doesn't do to think much, no."

The little boy who had come out threw himself at her lap: "Will there be *cohetes* at Christmas, *Tia?*"

"Yes, my darling."

"Rockets?" Carl asked.

"It is disgraceful. The men must have firearms to celebrate."

"Firearms!"

"Little rockets…"

"Ah, fire*works*!"

"To celebrate the Child's birth. But there are lovely things too, you shall see, at Christmas…"

"Don't talk like that!" the little boy ran at her.

"Ah, you are rude." She pushed him off gently. "This, speaking the English, is an indulgence of mine they cannot understand," she said to Carl.

"But you shall not give it up for that," he said.

She smiled. "Perhaps it is not a serious thing, like this farm. Until tomorrow, then," she said, standing up.

"*No mas! No mas!*" the child cried.

Carl stood. They walked in the house.

"You must take any book you wish," she said, indicating the low shelves under the sun porch window, another glass fronted case in the corner. "Of course, here, there are not so many as in the city." Carl crouched to look at the low shelves while she soothed the child: *Merck Veterinary Manual*, some engineering texts, Jack London, the complete works of Lin Yutang. He picked up one of these.

"He is one of your great philosophers I imagine," she said.

"I've never heard of him."

"Is that possible? I supposed he and Emerson…"

Carl was embarrassed" Ah, well, Emerson." What a strange misunderstanding. *Don* Rafa thought that Jack London was the greatest English writer. Lin Yutang. Perhaps it worked the other way too. "Tell me, is Páez one of your great writers?" he asked, thinking of the book he had found in the stable.

"Very great."

"Does every one agree?"

"No, many people object to Páez. There is Emerson here," she said, giving him a volume of essays in translation.

Orlando's wife came in then and claimed her for the kitchen. He took away the book. It was cuarto edition, published in Madrid. The pages were neatly sliced open to page 54.

THE DRY SEASON was lasting into the fourth month, though the storm clouds hung over the *cordillera*. The grass on the mountains burned palely in the daylight, leaving charred smudges above *Los Franceses*. At night you could see three fires in a row off to the west. When the rains came the slopes turned green in a day, Orlando said, and the cattle fed on the new grass. But the trees would not grow back, so the soil ran off and eventually the slope would turn barren and the only cactus would grow.

Generally the fires didn't approach the settlements, but one small village, Aguadas, had been moved out, Luciano said, and the nearest fire—the one above Los Franceses—burned down almost to their pasture, then ebbed.

CARL LAY under the mosquito net slitting the pages of his book with a kitchen knife.

"Why do you have to do that?" Blanche asked.

"It's quarto edition."

"Where do they publish books like that?"

Carl looked in the front of the book. "Barcelona."

"Oh, her books would be posh."

He didn't answer.

"What do you talk to your *doña* about?"

"I can't talk to her."

"Why not?"

"She doesn't know who I am."

"Who you are?"

He threw aside the book. "OH, we speak; but if we lived here fifty years she wouldn't know me. We haven't been properly introduced."

"You love her."

He didn't answer.

"Some kind of *mental* love, you're going to say."

"I didn't say anything."

"You give me a pain, Carl."

"I'm sorry."

"And us?"

"We are what we were."

"No, we aren't."

After he had fallen asleep, she got up and sat in the kitchen. The sound of Orlando's whistle approached down the hillside. She went out and watched him come into view in the light from a lantern on his stoop. He was wearing a rain poncho even though the rains were finished, carrying something inside it.

"What do you have?"

He opened the poncho and showed her: a little ocelot.

"Oh, I love him!" she said. "Where did you get him?"

"Up above. You have him. He is yours."

She took him and set him on the stoop. He began to lick his paws. "OH, see! A kitty cat, an ickle puddy!"

"They can get dangerous."

"No, no, he'll love me."

"Why should he?"

"Because I love him."

"Tell me something," He sat on the steps next to her. "You married to him in there?"

"No."

"I'm married. The *Doña* make us marry," he said.

"I know." Maybe you'll have a son. It's nice to have a son."

"I already have two."

"Where?"

"Down at. Kilómetro Veinticinco. Everywhere there is someone willing to give me a son. Except the ladies of the Christian Science. They give me Bible lessons…"

"Bible lessons?" Blanche was starting to giggle.

"Over there, in your country, I work for Christian Science Church. Handyman, that's me. They are good people. They take an interest in me. This lady who give me lessons, she was thirty-two; she does not believe in sex before marriage."

"Oh Gawd!" She put a hand over her mouth so as not to wake Carl.

"But everything, we do…everything; except for putting it in."

"Oh Jesus, God!"

"She love it, all the other things. 'Aye, Orlando!' she holler when I bring her. 'There is no one, no one like you…'"

"Stop, stop!" Blanche howled. "I'm wetting my…I'm wetting my pants!"

"She lick me, she bite me. Everything, everything but putting it in…"

"I'm wetting them. Oh, oh …" She stood up.

"*Asquerosa!*" He leaped away from her.

"Oh, my God, on my God! I haven't done that since eighth grade."

"*Puerca!*"

"Oh dear, oh dear!" she was dissolved.

"Fix yourself!" he yelled. "Don't just sit there!"

She jumped up and ran behind the bougainvillea, pulled off shorts and panties and flung them over the vine. "So what happened? The Bible lady?" she said, stepping into a pair of clean panties she'd hung to dry earlier.

"Oh, she drive me mad. I go mad. I have to smoke, drink. They take away my job; then I am good for nothing. I live on women. I am owing the telephone company, the electric company. They make me to leave. They deport me. Ach. I come back here and the *Doña* take care of me. Aye, women!" He stood up. I must go… My rounds. *Don* Rafa should not catch me here."

"And I can keep the kitty cat?" She buried her face in his fur.

"He is yours; but you can't trust them."

"No, he will love me. He will love me."

A DAY TOWARD the end of November, the *Doña* came up the hill with baskets. Carl went out to help her.

"No, no it is no matter. I will leave everything here for Orlando." She put two baskets down, held on to the other:

"Are you well? You look pale," she said. "Best to stay out of the sun."

"No, no. I am perfectly well." He walked beside her along the gravel path bordered by *margaritas*. They paused at a gardenia bush, and she stooped to pick off the browning flowers. The nephews were kicking a soccer ball about the courtyard, where Orlando's wife soaped the clothes. The ball rolled toward the girl, and she ran heavily after it and kicked it back.

"But, you must be careful," the *Doña* said, calling the girl over and pulling back her flying hair with a bit of ribbon she had in her pocket, then moving on.

"What is this?" he asked, pointing to a plant with shiny dark green leaves in the shape of broad spears.

"That is *columna*."

He took out a notebook and wrote the name together with a sketch of the leaf. Páez kept such notebooks he had read.

"It is also called *Rubona*. It has no flower, but its leaf is handsome."

"Yes, yes, handsome."

"It likes shade. That's why I've put it here under the fig tree. I think that it is one of the little plants I dug up in the rain forest between Cata and the beach at Novilleros. I was afraid it might be too warm for it here, but it's done well." She looked at him gravely: "You wished to speak to me about something?"

"Well, there is the matter of a pig...Willi asked if I would speak to you. He would like us to buy a sow to mate."

"Ah, pigs are a trouble. We used to have pigs. It was before *don* Rafa's illness."

"He was ill?"

"Many years."

"I didn't know." He did know; Orlando had told them, but he didn't like to reveal how much Orlando had revealed.

"He used to speak of it as a cosmic pessimism," she said. "It began fifteen years ago. He had to retire for a number of years... Yet I think it started earlier, his...not to be able to decide..."

"...ran away the day of his wedding," Orlando had said. Everybody knew about it, but she," ...took a market bus to La Viga; his cousins found him there in one of the bars behind the potato sacks, brought him back an hour and a half late, and an excuse was made and the wedding went on...*She* was the only one didn't know, or maybe she did ," Orlando told them.

"The trouble, his trouble..."

"Not being able to decide," Carl helped her.

"Yes, it got worse," she said. "Became illness. He would wake up in the morning and not be able to decide if he should put his shirt on first, or shave, or whether to dress at all. So it was he remained in his pajamas all day, pacing the floor.

"Only the ancient game of *tute* could soothe him. We would play it all morning, he and I; then the widow of Pepe Tirado who lived in the apartment below would be good enough to come up in the afternoons to play. To this day I cannot look at a playing card. He would not learn a new game, no matter how we begged. Nothing new, nothing unfamiliar.

"He would read, but always a book he had read before. Spengler, over and over. I sometimes thought The *Decline of the West* was somehow related to our own decline!" She gave a little laugh.

"But he recovered...?"

"Yes, it was a miracle. I had a young nephew studying medicine in Paris. One day he came home on his vacation and gave him some new pill. It cured him in a week. The whole town spoke of it as a miracle.

"He went back to his office, he went out to cafes again, and took an interest in politics. We came up here and he began raising pigs, chickens. The man you know."

"Yes."

She straightened up, placing the *margaritas* she had picked in the basket. A pig, yes, we shall see."

"It would be our responsibility. It's care, I mean."

"Yes, of course. A pig is a great care. One used to be slaughtered every year for Christmas."

"El *puerco conocido*," he said.

"Ah, yes," she laughed: "The pig one is acquainted with. I would never acquaint myself with a pig that I may later, how you say? Roast." She handed him some of the margaritas. "Your wife will like?"

"Yes, thank you. You are so good...so..."

"A quite ordinary woman," she said firmly.

"No, not ordinary, not ordinary. I...think..."

"Please."

"I think of you. You are always in my..."

"No, no!"

"Please, I must. I...I admire you. I admire you in the most extraordinary way."

"But you must not."

"Oh, God, oh God! Forgive me!"

"It would be wise to go in," she said. "The sun..."

"Your baskets..."

"Orlando will take them."

"Forgive me."

"It is no matter."

He followed her:" if you would just allow me to explain. I don't mean to upset you..."

"Please." She put a hand on his arm and he caught it up in his.

"No, no!"

He released her. "Forgive me, forgive me."

"We will not speak of it more." She moved toward the house.

"I can say it better, if you will allow me."

"No, no, you must not!"

"I...I think how everything here..." he gestured around him."...how everything you touch . you care for...I think, just let me...just let me be one of these things you care for, like this garden..."

"You must not speak this way."

"How can I help? How can one help?"

"One can always help."

"I mean if you knew. If you knew how my mind goes around, how I cannot help observing how no one *sees* you as I do. Oh, I know how this sounds, how arrogant."

"Arrogant, yes; God sees. It is for God to see."

"Oh, God! Don't talk of God. I mean who is it says I cannot feel this way? Is it God?"

"I must go in," she said.

"Forgive me, then, at least that. Let us be like before."

She smiled. "You have a young wife."

"Yes, yes." He had been tempted to tell her they were not married, but it would have shocked her. Or, he wondered, would it have tempted her to force them before a priest? But no, he thought bitterly, she didn't even care enough for that.

"I shall speak to don Rafa about the pig. One must go in now, out of the sun." She picked up the basket.

HE MADE A NEW RESOLVE and found it gave him some peace. I will *watch* her, he thought. No one will know it. I will simply watch her. He imagined this watching as something which might happen over an uncounted number of years. It would be a focus for his life.

He was very careful of her for a week. The lessons became as before. She didn't invite him to walk in the garden, though she was as cordial as ever when they had the coffee and buns after the lesson. He had noted that she went every Thursday with Juan the driver in the car, carrying with her baskets full of canned goods and some fruits from the trees. Finally he asked if he might go with her. She hesitated, then consented; so the following Thursday he was ready when Juan brought out the baskets.

"But they will tire you, my little visits," said *doña* Luz. They can be of no interest to a young man like you. I leave my little baskets with these poor people and is discussed when the rains will come."

"I wish to go," Carl repeated, helping her put into each basket the cellophane bags of Fideos Lux, the black beans, the jars of fig preserves, the string bags of bitter local oranges and limes, the boxes of *petits beurres*.

"You will not speak again of the matters you…the other day."

"No, no, never again," he said.

Juan drove them, down to Kilometro Veintitres, behind the *telefónico*, a rutted track which threaded a narrow canyon and climbed halfway up the opposite slope, where they got out and walked, the baskets carried by Juan and six or seven little boys who clamored: "LA *Doña*, vine La *Doña*."

The first shack was that of an aged woman tended by a mute boy. The basket was placed on the stoop and emptied by the boy. *Bendita mujer*," said the woman. Her eyes were filmed over; she seemed to have only sidelong vision, in which she held the *Doña*. .

"Give them the Coca Cola," the woman said to the boy, and he held a bottle out to Carl, who stood uncomfortably in the dusty yard finishing the warm flat drink as the boy stood watching him as if administering a dose. *Doña* Luz refused hers, asking instead for a cutting of an unusual philodendron rooting in a pail on the stoop.

Walking on, with the little plant wrapped in her handkerchief, she warned him to ask for juice if they wanted to bring him a drink, not Coca Cola; it was too expensive.

Doña, Mercedes, in the next cottage, expected them to enter and sit on two rusted chrome chairs, either side of a glass-topped coffee table on which was an arrangement of flowers. The floor was swept earth; and, high on one whitewashed wall, hung an oleograph of the Sacred Heart.

"*Mi hija menor*," said *doña* Mercedes, indicating the pretty girl sitting on a brocade settee next to a young man." And Gonzalo, her sweetheart." Gonzalo stood up and offered a hand to Carl. The girl sat mute through the introduction. She was dressed up in a three-piece outfit.

"He is from Cartago," said the mother, meaning the young man.

"Ah, Cartago," said the *Doña*, accepting a glass of *badea* pulp and a cracker from a *cellophane* pack. "We pass through Cartago coming from Las Marias. There is a place in the Paseo Bedout where we stop to eat sausages." A bit of cracker fell from her lap and

she bent over to recover it from the earth floor.

She is a lady, thought Carl. She passes the ultimate test of ladyhood, making this polite talk in this appalling place.

"There is the sugar mill as well," said *doña* Mercedes.

"I work in the sugar mill," said the young man.

"He repairs tractors," said *doña* Mercedes.

The girl said nothing. She was elaborately painted and sat as if not to disturb the fall of her taffeta skirt.

"They will marry in February," said *doña* Mercedes.

"I congratulate you."

"Will you have a Coke?" the woman inquired of Carl.

"No, no!"

"The rains are delayed this year."

"Yes, yes, *don* Rafael was commenting just this morning."

Carl stared at the barbed and bleeding heart of Christ hung high on the opposite wall. A child ran through the room. "My grandson," said the woman of the house. Luz Elena's child."

"So sweet," said the *Doña*.

"Gonzalo is an expert in electrical relays."

"Gonzalo straightened up his shoulders: "I have train at the Polytechnic," he said in English to Carl.

"He is young man with much future," said the mother.

"It is a fine thing," said *doña* Luz.

"Yes, they will do well. They will have a house with French provincial…"

"A lovely girl," said Carl's lady.

The girl merely smiled slightly through all this. Women, here, found their voices only in middle age, Carl thought. He watched the *Doña* fondle the child, felt stifled. How does she bear it? Couldn't she simply send Juan around with the baskets?

They went on. A crippled woman with three infants had no oleographs on the wall, or plastic flowers on the table. The single room contained two rusted cots, a petroleum stove, a table covered in oilcloth, and two benches.

"The pain is terrible, *Doña*. I walk all bent over." Her spine was twisted, causing the hip on which the youngest child rode to protrude grotesquely.

"Dr. Escobar Soto will see you. He is my own doctor."

But what could he do about this? What can anyone do? Carl thought.

"You take the silver bus, I believe, from the…"

"Oh, I know about buses, *Doña*."

Carl emptied the basket on to one of the benches. Here there was nothing to admire.

They left, climbed the rest of the way up the hill by a narrow track. At least twenty children trailed them now. "These next you will find rather educated people. They are exiles, from over the border. Don Sergio is an organizer of strikes. Sonia teaches in the school."

They entered a tiny house that was whitewashed inside and out, with gauze curtains in the windows to keep out flies. A robust young woman embraced *doña* Luz and shook Carl's hand: "Sergio is not here." This seemed a relief to *doña* Luz. She took a seat; at a metal table where two children studied.

"Greet the *Doña* nicely," said Sonia. Girl and boy stood up and gave their hands to *doña* Luz and to Carl.

"*Y usted…*" she said to Carl, her face full of humor. "We have heard about you." She brought them coffee, sitting down herself and pulling her coarse black hair away from her face, which was also coarse but pleasant. Unlike the *Doña*, Carl thought, she is sure of being a good woman; her children sit before her, obviously healthy, polite, studious.

"They are spreading tacks on the road today, in support of the truckers," Sonia said. "You must tell Juan to tie twigs in front of the wheels,"

"Today?"

"Yes, they were around last night, between here and La Verenjena. Didn't you notice?"

"Nothing."

"David," she said to the boy. "Go tell Juan." The boy ran.

"So," she said to Carl," What do you think of us here?"

He wasn't prepared for her directness. "It's all very new," he said. "I am very interested…"

"Nothing is new to me," she said. "It is all the same as before. I never knew if he comes home. Yet we are well here. They accept my certificate. I am paid full salary now. And my brother comes and will add to the house, two rooms, a kitchen and a room for himself. He's a quiet man. He'll come home evenings."

"You're a good woman, Sonia," said the *Doña*.

"Yes…though I don't baptize my children. I know you are thinking that."

"Perhaps, if one is frank, yes."

Carl noted the absence of oleographs. The only things to hang on the wall were a machete and one of the carved wooden chocolate beaters that came from Tula.

"I am aware that a wife must obey a husband," said *doña* Luz gently. "This is a delicious coffee."

It was delicious, and Carl drank it with guiltless pleasure.

"Our own beans. We sell, now, the eggs as well. We have enough to sell. Will you see?" She led them out to the yard. Under a mango tree was a coop made of derelict boards, covered with scraps of Eternit roofing, on which were spread coffee beans. A garden was also enclosed in boards. Carl wondered why. He'd never seen any wild animals about, never a squirrel, or even a rabbit.

Sonia handed him a large egg. "Duck," she said. "You have to get used to them." Carl, who had bought one by mistake in the market and found it bad tasting, put it in his pocket, followed the two women up a hill, Sonia's strong calves just in front of him. "My place," she said when they reached the top. There was a bench and an arbor of woodroses. They sat down, Carl on the ground, at the feet of *doña* Luz.

"You see the valley from here," Sonia said. "All the way to Kilómetro Diez y ocho."

"But it's lovely," said *doña* Luz, clapping her hands. "Truly!"

"Sergio laughs at me. 'Here, I come and pray you will not be killed,' I tell him. 'I lose, through you, my family, my homeland, my religion. I can at least pray they do not take you.'"

"My dear," said *doña* Luz.

"I will be strong, yes, I will. He will come home tonight, like all other nights."

"Yes, of course."

"It will be some other day, some ordinary day when I am not expecting it, he won't come."

"No, no, you mustn't say such things." The *Doña* embraced her while she sat straight and still, her eyes closed.

"Forgive me, please."

"My dear."

Sonia wiped her eyes with her apron, and led them back down the hill. "I thank you for your visit," she said, and gave them two papayas. Her face was empty, now and calm. She gave Carl her hand. "You come again."

"I will," he said, "With much pleasure!"

Juan had tied brushes of twigs in front of each tire. Some of the trucks they passed had devised the same safeguard. Several were of the road with blowouts.

A PAIR OF HAMPSHIRE PIGS was purchased. Male and female. They were sleek and black with a white belt running down both front legs. Willi pointed out the tightly curled tails and the bright little eyes, signs of health. He had learned something of pigs when he spent summers with his uncle. They would be mated, and the male sacrificed at Christmas. Willi built them a fenced yard behind the stable, and no attempt was made to become acquainted with them except by Blanche, who liked to lean over the boards and tickle the sow with a branch from a coffee bush. *Don Rafa* bought a new notebook and hung it on a nail to record their weight gain. The male weighed 172 pounds and the female, 160 pounds. By Christmas, it was hoped the male would be close to 250. They ate the leftover tortillas and the eggshells from breakfast and drank milk mixed with *agua panela*. At night Willi boiled up a mash for them on the kerosene stove. If the mating took, there would be tender piglet to roast by next July according to Willi's calculations.

The rains held off, however, and Willi worried about the cistern. He had to leave off the pigs' daily bath with Orvus soap. The bruised clouds hung back behind the *cordillera,* and fires crisped the dry mountainsides.

A morning when Carl was reading with *doña* Luz, the girl Miriam announced that there was a Virgin on the mountainside.

"*Pero qué!*" exclaimed the *Doña*, starting up from her chair.

"You see it from here," said Miriam, motioning them to the center of the patio. "No, no, you don't. From the kitchen patio better." They followed her through the kitchen to the washing patio at the back of the house. "There," she pointed. "I saw her first." It was the most Carl had ever heard her speak.

"Above the *Franceses*, on the track to Palomares," said Olga, her hands deep in corn *masa*. The fires will take her, they're saying," she added.

"Who is saying?" asked *doña* Luz.

"Down below, at Kilometro Veinte. A priest has been sent for."

Carl squinted against the sun. Something bluish, tent shaped, moving slightly in the wind; though there was no wind there below...

"It is a hysteria," said *don* Rafa, discovering them.

"It isn't clear, obviously it's something," the *Doña* said.

"A Pisanista flag, left over from the last election," said *don* Rafa.

"Away up there, *mi hijo?* Who would carry such a thing up there? There isn't even a path."

"Ah, one never knows with Pisanistas. With them it is always extremes," said *don* Rafa.

"If one could only see clearer. The opera glasses Carlina left you, have we them somewhere?" asked the *Doña*.

"They have looked with a glass already, up at the *Franceses*. You do not see clearer, only larger," stated Olga.

"*Pero qué diablos!*" norte *don* Rafa.

"I think in the drawer with your socks. I'll just have a little look." *Doña* Luz went into the house.

"Some people were going up there with *Padre* Elias from San Fernando," said Olga. "But they are afraid...the fire."

"A hysteria," said *don* Rafa, "Pure hysteria."

The *Doña* returned with the opera glasses; and, after taking a long look, handed them to *don* Rafa:

"A little look, here, a flag, I will wager; yes, a flag; it is quite clear; a blue Pisanista flag."

Doña Luz took back the glasses, refocused them silently. Finally, she said: "It isn't clear, as Olga says; it does seem to turn and..."

"Yes, it turns," said Olga, "And walks a way up the mountain, you see!"

"The flag, it is blowing in the wind," said *don* Rafa.

"There is no wind," said Olga stolidly.

"Up there, there is a wind; the flag is blowing in the wind; that is the motion you... here, we shall ask our gringo here." He handed the glasses to Carl." He has no interest either way. He will approach the matter in a cool, scientific way. Look, you; very fine opera glasses from Paris."

Carl focused the glasses on the mountainside. The shape swept close, and for a moment he saw what might have passed for a Virgin; but the truth was it wasn't clear, larger, but not clearer.

"So?" said *don* Rafa.

"It could be a flag and it could be a figure," Carl said to everyone's dissatisfaction. "That is, it's blue, it moves."

"There, you see, an objective statement. The scientific mind," said *don* Rafa. In this country we have not the scientific mind."

"A scientist," said Orlando, who had come in with the milk, "would go up there with *Padre* Elias and see."

"*Padre* Elias, ha ha! *Padre* Elias has in his mind to see a Virgin, he'll see a Virgin if has to hallucinate!" whooped *don* Rafa.

After supper, *don* Rafa brought out a bottle of Cruz Verde:

"To the scientific impulse, eh?" he said, tossing off a glassful.

"*Bueno el Cruz Verde, no?*"

"*Bien bueno*," said Orlando.

"I have a taste for it since I walked those passes up there," *don* Rafa gestured with the bottle toward the Cordillera Central, "Surveying the route of that railroad that never went through. Aye the *maldita* railroad of *don* Roque Villegas; it was going to make the legislators of Valencia rich as thieves. We used to sit on the verandah of the Hotel Caracas in Belén drinking Ron Viejo to warm the gut. The mists didn't rise off the mountains till eleven in the morning. What a country, what a country! Place where ~ Judas lost he boots, eh? And now we have this Virgin, ach!"

"It is odd," Carl said'.

"What's that?"

"How it's not clearer with the glasses."

"Hah! Now we have our Gringo corrupted by kitchen maids, by my old lady."

"But…you shouldn't"

"Shouldn't…?"

"Speak of her…in that way."

"Ah, hah!" Don Rafa examined him closely in the lamplight. "So, you are an admirer of my wife, eh? So, yes, yes, my wife is one of the, shall we say, *flowerings* of our feudal state. One must admire her, but one must look also at the state. One can admire her, but must look also at the understructure, at what is bearing her up, so to speak: a lot of poor devils carrying loads on their backs, eh? You must know that."

"Well, if you speak of that; what is bearing one up, what is bearing anyone up? What is bearing me up?" Carl stammered. "Wars, wars, legitimized industrial greed." His face flamed.

"Ah, now, one chooses, one chooses one's guilt. Your 'legitimized industrial greed', I'm sure it produces some charming ladies too."

"Never, never anyone like her," Carl said.

"So, you have experienced them all! Hah, but I must tell you something about my lady. She is my first cousin. We marry so the money stays in the family." *Don* Rafa poured another round. "Well, tell me then what is so extraordinary that you find?"

"I can't explain."

"Ah, it is some kind of mystery! Mysteries, Virgins. To be a reactionary at your age. How old are you?"

"Twenty-five."

"Twenty-five. At twenty-five, as I've told you, I was plotting assassinations."

"I'm not political," Carl said. "I've told you."

Don Rafa wandered outside the circle of the lantern, returned:

"Tell me then, what is this something you find in *doña* Luz, in this ferrous piece of mountainside she married to keep in the family?"

"Chartres Cathedral…" Carl began.

"*Diós*! Chartres Cathedral!"

"Chartes Cathedral, the south door, the Virgin lies on the ground.

"More Virgins!" *Don* Rafa lit a cigarette in the dark.

"…Low, lowly, a carpenter's wife. She's given birth in straw."

"An astonishing young man you are…"

"But at the same time she's a queen. That was their notion: a Queen of Heaven, Mistress of the Seven…"

"Aye! A medieval young man!"

"Mistress of the Seven Liberal Arts."

"Chartres Cathedral, yes that was another matter. Our virgins, though, our virgins are worn out." *Don* Rafa waved toward the mountain: "That, that up there, if it is a virgin, it's an old dead battery, an old dead battery of a virgin!"

"The rains will save her," Orlando said from his place on the stoop.

"The rains, yes." *Don* Rafa came back into the circle of light.

"They are coming. You see the clouds over the Pico Coqui," Orlando said.

"Yes; late, but they are coming."

"The people down below say they come to save the Virgin, that God will not allow the fires to take her," said Orlando.

"Ha ha ha! The Virgin or the Pisanista flag!" burst from don Rafa. The Virgin or the Pisanista flag!"

CARL BROUGHT WILLI to meet Sonia. They rode up on the afternoon bus. Willi was eager to meet the family.

"This woman is a teacher, you say?"

"Yes."

"It's your intellectual proletariat. Teachers here, I'm told, only make menial wage. Their only resource is revolution."

"I don't think Sonia is that political."

"You say that her husband was laying tacks?"

"Yes, a trucker's strike. He warned us to tie some brushes in front of the tires."

"And they have some crops."

"Yes. The coffee crop looked to be farther along than ours. Also the tomatoes. And a whole hillside of cabbages."

"So it is all there…"

"What?"

"The Maoist elements. The agricultural base. The political awareness."

Willi's excitement reminded Carl of Carl Marx's desire to encounter a German Socialist.

He watched out the window of the bus for the nearest stop where they could get out and walk up the hill to the farm. As he remembered it was just beyond Kilometro Treinta where Juan had turned off and headed up a rutted road as far as the Mercedes would go. Yes, here was the little crossroads, with the pharmacy and the telephone exchange with the lottery agency and the little *abasto* in front, the whole place even smaller and more miserable than their own little village.

They got off too soon and had to walk a mile or so further on the main road before they found the turn off.

They found Sergio at home that day, sorting coffee beans with his son. Sonia gripped Carl's hand and smiled. "You see he came," she said.

"I'm very glad."

Sergio got a bottle of Ron Viejo from the kitchen and brought it out to the table on the front porch. He was a square, sturdy man like his wife, his smooth, beardless face reddened over the cheekbones by the altitude. The girl, Concha, sat at the table with them, frowning over a geometry lesson.

"So, you stay with *don* Rafa, eh? I have met him. One of the old Liberals. One of the Great Talkers. They couldn't even kill El Cóndor. We have done with all that," said Sergio.

"How is that?" Willi asked after Carl had translated Sergio's words for him.

"The mountain, the mountain will defeat the plain. Here in the *cordillera* is our future, our party, our leaders. The city cannot corrupt them. We wait. We are good at waiting. But we prepare…

"Listen, listen, I will show you. Come." He got up and led them through a small back room and out through the dusty back yard, past the chicken coop of derelict boards and up the hill Carl had climbed before with Sonia's strong calves before him. Just behind the arbor of veranera—Sonia's praying place—the cliff rose sharply. Sergio parted a thicket of vine, pulled: away a pallet of weathered boards over which a mesh of dead branches had been stapled. Behind, a tunnel had been dug into the red clay.

Sergio pulled out a crate and pried it open. It was filled with rifles wrapped in rags.

"M-14s," he said, unwrapping the greasy cloth. "Fires 7.62 millimeter cartridges; has a range up to seven hundred meters. And this." He dug out another. "Grenade launcher. Aluminum barrel. Has a range between a hand grenade and a mortar, can destroy a machine gun emplacement or troop concentration within four hundred meters and it's easy to use."

He pulled out another crate and unwrapped a pair of machine guns." M16's, modified for automatic fire. And these: Russian AKM's semi-automatic. Thirty round magazines."

"Where do you get them?" Willi asked.

"The AKM's come in the powdered milk."

"What?"

"The Centros Rurales receive aid shipments. I tell you this, show you all this, because you are *fugitivos* like us. Isn't that true?"

"Yes, yes," Willi said.

"I take the risk of trusting you, right?"

"Yes, yes, you can trust us."

"The rice and the milk are sent in from Eastern Europe, then they are distributed by the Rurales. Presently, these weapons, which we dig out of the sacks, are hidden in caves in thirty-four districts. We avoid concentrations of weapons, same as we avoid troop concentrations. It is a disseminated focus. We go on with our lives, with our farming; but there are periods of training. We have seventeen *focos*. I am the leader of ours. We are the closest to the city. It is, here, most dangerous to operate.

"Some weapons come also from the *cuartel*," Sergio said, rewrapping the machine guns in rags. "Sabotage, desertions take place. We surrounded a company on maneuvers a month ago, took over a hundred M-16's and a dozen or so grenade launchers. Since then we've had to be very careful. They took reprisals, shot up a billiard hall." He pushed away the crate of weapons, pulled out a cardboard box: "My books."

Carl knelt to look. There was *The Marx Engels Reader*, Gorki's *La Madre*, paperbacks of Debray, a quarto edition of Zola's *Germinal* on creamy paper like the *Doña's* books.

"I must hide them now. It becomes more dangerous." Sergio pushed the boxes back in and straightened up. "You were right to leave there," he said. "It is because of that that I show you this. It is all one struggle, yes?"

"Yes, yes," Willi nodded.

They walked back down the hill. "You say nothing, especially to *don* Rafa. He is a good man. He was in prison in the days of Salazar they say. It is only, he talks, and the time for that is over.

"'The urge to destroy is also the creative urge,' Bakunin said. The Liberal's parliamentary democracy is nothing but a fraud, a clever instrument which the middle class would use to dominate the masses. These gentlemen we have now in the Palacio de Armas will perpetuate themselves until the devil knows…

"Azarin Salazar, who is minister of justice, has been president twice before and it will be thrown his way again. His father was president three times. He put together a private army to kill strikers."

They walked back down the hill and sat under a silkcotton tree with the bottle of Ron Viejo.

"Our other weapon is the strikes. But this we must leave mostly to our brothers in the city. At the end, though, at the end, we will all come together as it was in Petrograd, the militia handing their weapons to the strikers. It must ripen, it must ripen."

"You have a good soil here," Willi said, nudging at an anthill with his sandal.

"Yes, volcanic ash. Better than over your way. Yes, we will have a good harvest. Life is good. My children grow; my wife has her profession; but one lives for ideas or one is a brute."

"Ach! Ideas!" cried Sonia, who stooped nearby, sorting coffee beans.

"For justice, *mi amor*," he said.

She bent over her beans, not answering.

THE BRUISED CLOUDS remained just behind the mountains and the rains didn't come, but the Virgin remained, untouched. "Run, see, Olga," *doña* Berta said every afternoon at cards.

"See if she's still there."

"Still up there, eh, turning the heads of kitchen girls," said *don* Rafa, sitting on their stoop. "You get this talk of miracles when a religion is new and when it's in decay. A compound in putrefaction gives up its elements. It's simple chemistry. It all begins in miracles and goes out in miracles." Carl sat staring up at the fires. Willi sucked a lime.

"Only the other day it as in the papers: stone turned up holding down the morning edition of *El Pais* in a Las Marias doorway. Boy who's selling the papers suffers one of those fungal infestations that eat away the limb, suffering it like fate as they do here, the unwashed. Well, Suddenly, it starts to clear up, the sores. Boy takes it into his head the stone cured him. It's examined. Turns out there are some marks on it. Seems it's a piece off an ancient Mayan sculpture. Well, next thing you know, there's a roadside shrine, medicine men consulted, bishops convened, headlines daily."

"And the boy?"

"The boy? I don't recall. Probably he's being drawn about in a cart with his limb on display. Or forgotten. It's understandable the boy's forgotten. *La miseria, pues,* everyone's for forgetting that."

"But who's to do something!" Carl erupted.

"Yes, we talk. Years, we talked, I admit. Precious little we did. Best to shut up. My wife distributes her baskets; I suppose that's something."

"Trouble is," said Willi, "No one's seen what could be made of it ."

"Of what?" asked don Rafa. *La miseria?* What can be made of it but more misery

"No, no, limits, possessing only what's necessary. Where do the diminishing returns begin in possessing? Knowing.that."

"Ah, well, asceticism. It's an elite understands such things."

"But must that be so?"

"You give money to one of these *miserables*. Does he spend it on wholesome food or necessities? No, he shows off with a banquet, spends it all on drink and *bizcochos*," said *don* Rafa.

"Maybe the fault lies in the money," Willi said.

"How so?"

"Money creates diffuse desires, unreality," Willi said.

"But how are we to do away with it? It's there and everyone wants it," Carl asked.

"By faith,"

"Faith in what?"

"In this lime," Willi said, holding one up. "In its reality, it's nourishment, its beauty. There's no use hoarding it; it will spoil."

"And who's to be prophet of this faith?"

"It's prophet will come. For every truth, there's never lacked a prophet."

"You're right about faith of course," said *don* Rafa. Nothing's ever accomplished without passion. We're an age short of passion, of symbol; whatever's up there…Virgin, well she's dying; Pisanista flag, well they lost in '59. I carried their banner through the streets once myself. Pisano inspired a certain...an honest man, you know, you had to call him that. Bad stammer. Poignant that he'd stand up in public at all, put himself forward. Proposed alternating power with the opposition. You need to know the history to appreciate that. Decades of mass murder in the countryside. Liberals, Conservatives slitting each other's throats. He'd open the jails. 'The forgiving has to start somewhere;' he said, barely able to spit the words out. You had to admire. He lost in '61, again in '64. In '65, he made the mistake of accepting communist support, and lost even the nomination."

"But what's the answer?" Carl cried.

"Answer? If we live the other side of a veil?" said *don* Rafa.

THREE HENS DIED the first week in December. "Why do they die?" Blanche asked Carl when he came up from burying the last one in the plantain grove. She had doused herself with water from the spigot and lay on the grassy verge in her bathing suit.

"The zinc roof. It heats up."

"I don't know what kind of a farm this is. Nothing but flowers and sick hens and an old cow, and *her* staring, standing in the sun hatching her baby. I could do that. I'd like to do that…"

"Don't be stupid."

"Don't *you* be stupid."

"We agreed we didn't want a child."

"I can't remember. Why didn't we?"

"The world, the way it is."

"The world? When was the world ever different, I'd like to know? When did it ever stop people having …? Oh, Carl...!" She was crying.

"You're so unhappy?"

"If you loved me…"

"We belong to each other. What must I say?"

"There's her. I see you with her."

"She's old; as you say. Why should you worry?"

"I don't know. I don't know anything anymore."

THEN, IN THE NIGHT, the first week in December, about three weeks late, the rains finally came. Willi heard the drumming on the zinc roof and thought of the cistern filling, of the pigs having their baths again and becoming sleek. Life was good, as Sergio said.

The mountains turned green again in a matter of hours it seemed. The Virgin was saved, supposedly, but they all stopped looking up at her, and one day she wasn't there anymore.

Chapter 3

On a day in the second week of December, just after the morning storm, one of the children of the storekeeper below came up with a message from Sonia: would don Will and don Carl come to her at the abasto without saying anything to anyone? They walked down the hill and found her alone in the little room behind the store:

"You will come with me and talk to him, please, un *Norteamericano*."

"North American...?"

"They have kidnapped him and brought him to us," she said.

"What? Who?"

"Our people in the city. They have kidnapped him. A rich *norteamericano*. He is a vice-president of a company. He is sick, dying maybe. It seems he wishes to die. You must talk to him. We cannot. He does not understand. You will see. There is a bus in an hour. You will return with me, and come back on the morning bus?"

"Yes, yes, of course," Willi said.

They sat and drank *aguardiente* in the back room, while Sonia sent one of the children back to tell Blanche they would be away until late. There was a bus back at eleven o'clock.

"We learned from the newspapers he is a diabetic," Sonia went on. "We have sent for insulin, a doctor. He has been in the *cordillera* for three weeks without insulin. It was too far. There were no doctors, so they brought him secretly to us. He is very weak; we must hurry. They are asking a quarter of a million dollars for his return. Our liaison says they are willing to pay. He is a vice-president, as I told you. The negotiations are going forward, but we must keep him alive."

"But what must we say to him?" Carl asked.

"That he must let the doctor examine him, test his urine; that he must let us give him the injections."

"Yes, yes."

"That his company wishes to save him, wishes to pay the money. You will say nothing of this to anyone?"

"No, no, of course!"

"Always before we have returned these men alive. It is because of this they pay our ransoms."

The bus came. They got on and sat at the front. Two farmers and a woman with a chicken in her arms sat at the back; the rest of the bus was empty. Sonia leaned close to speak in whispers: "It has never been our experience they die for their companies, you know. We don't know what is the matter with him; perhaps he is depressed."

"Yes, probably."

"The doctor is risking much to come, but he is willing. He is one of us."

The bus roared along the Carretera al Mar for five kilometers, took the turnoff to Candelaria.

"Dangerous for you too," Will said.

"Yes. We have lived with it so long."

At Candelara, the bus bucked up a steep hill, down a narrow, rutted way past the *galeria central* and a whitewashed church. The woman with the chicken got off. They circled a tiny plaza. Music of Luis Berrios blared from a *cantina*. They took the narrow road to Kilómetro Treinta.

When they got off, a fine rain had begun, and Sonia pulled a poncho out of her string bag, held it over them as they climbed the path to the house.

THEY HAD GIVEN Paul Seybolt their bedroom. He lay on the cheap chenille spread, his face flushed though the day was cool. He was wearing chinos and a tennis shirt, both quite dirty. Willi sat on a bench at the far end of the little room. Carl stood in the doorway with Sonia. Sergio stayed in the kitchen.

"We speak English," Willi said.

The man said nothing.

Willi moved closer: "Why won't you let a doctor see you?"

"Good God!" laughed the man." What next?"

"You're a diabetic?" Carl asked.

"So, you've been reading about me in the newspapers."

"We know they wish to return you alive, that things are going forward. Your company wishes to…"

"Who, precisely, are you?" Paul Seybolt said, looking at Carl.

"No one, really," Carl shrugged.

"What are you doing in this place?"

"A little of this and that," Willi said. "That's not the point."

"Ah, yes, 'No one really,' 'A little of this and that.' I have a son wants to be no one really. Sleep therapy, they're trying. Ever hear of that?"

Seybolt lay with his eyes closed. He seemed to have exhausted himself. When he began speaking again, it was in such a weak voice they had to come close to the bed.

"I was co-founder of this company they're demanding quarter of a million from; did the newspapers say that?"

"I don't know," Carl said. "We didn't see the papers."

There was no reply.

"He will not eat," Sonia said. "He hasn't eaten for two days. "There was perspiration odor in the room, foot odor.

"Fourteen hour days we used to put in." Paul Seybolt found the strength to say. "I

was worth a quarter million then. Used to make our products in a barn. My first child slept on the floor in a basket. Those were the good days, yes."

"And then?" Carl asked.

"Then, the big time. When we first came down here, company put us up in the Tucuman-Sheraton for four months while my wife searched for a house had enough

style for us. You think that didn't cost…?"

"You're depressed," Willi said.

"Yes, depressed. Do you blame me? Let me finish."

"Go on."

"Even then, I was worth something to us. Then I had a heart attack; my son was put to sleep for three weeks to cure his maladjustment. We were in the hands of doctors. Pills to sleep, pills to wake up. Then my wife left me. Took the children and went to live on her father's ranch in California. I live alone in a twenty-room house. I can only go in to work fifteen hours a week, the doctors tell me. Diminishing returns…"

"Your company wishes to pay."

"In the hands of doctors." The voice was weakening.

"Listen, man, they want to return you alive!" Willi shouted.

"They have their wants and I have mine," said Paul Seybolt, falling back on the pillow.

"You want to die?" Willi asked.

"Probably I do, yes." Seybolt took a couple deep breaths, then said, "Tell me, are you one of these?"

"We are friends," Willi said.

"Ah, friends. Yes. Yes, probably I will die. It doesn't matter. They chose the wrong man, tell them. A lemon, tell them." He closed his eyes.

"You will not let a doctor...?"

"No, no doctor."

Carl went in the kitchen where Sergio was. "Can you have the injections given forcibly?"

"Perhaps. The pharmacist gave me a kit to test the urine and we took some from him when Sergio got him up to the bathroom. He tried to spill it but we saved most of it."

"The pharmacist also is one of us," said Sergio."

"How soon can the money be found?"

"They are still negotiating. It may take two weeks."

"He will not cooperate."

"No, what we were afraid of."

They sat at the kitchen table and had meat pies with hot chocolate. The rain continued and there were several bursts of thunder and lightning strikes close by. "I think there is more to treating him than just insulin," Sonia said. "I think there are matters about diet. He asks for *aguardiente* but will not eat."

Willi, who had eaten three meat pies, took another and went in the bedroom and held it out to the man on the bed. He waved it away and closed his eyes.

Sonia cleared the table and set out a bottle of rum. The children worked on geometry problems at the foot of the table under the oil lamp. At about nine-thirty, the doctor came: a frightened man in his sixties, fussing over a split umbrella. He had been contacted by telegram and had never before in his life received a telegram, he told them. "Have you brought the insulin?" Sonia asked, serving him a cup of chocolate.

"Yes. I could hardly decipher the message. I was so flustered. Have you the urine? They told me they gave you a kit."

"Yes." Sonia brought the urine in a preserve jar. The doctor dipped a tape in it:

"You must do this twice a day. If the green patch turns brown, as you see here, increase the insulin injections. Then, this pink patch…if it darkens, there is a ketosis. You must give extra feedings—rice is best. I will write this down." He took out a pad and sat down at the table to write.

"Who is to give the injection?" asked the doctor.

"I," said Sonia.

"Do you know how?"

"Yes," she said. "I learned at the *Rurales*."

"We can begin with forty units in the morning. If the patch turns brown at noon orso, give another twenty in the evening ." He stopped writing, mopped the sweat off his face. "I sincerely doubt, I sincerely doubt you can handle this."

"We must handle it," said Sonia.

"Is he eating?"

"Very little."

"Thirsty?"

"Yes.",

"No sweets."

"Of course, of course; we know that."

"He's four plus," the doctor said, comparing the little tab to a chart on the side of the bottle, "But no ketosis so far. Simply giving insulin is not the entire solution. You have insulin shock to avoid. He becomes weak and perspires, extremely hungry, you must give sugar water and hold the injection."

"Yes, yes, I understand," Sonia said.

They went in the bedroom and held him down while the doctor observed Sonia give the injection. It was easy; there was no strength in him, Carl observed as he held the shoulders. The doctor examined his eyes and feet. There was an infected toenail. "That's bad. Use this Betadine solution I'll leave you, three times a day, and keep it elevated. Could lose the foot you don't take care."

They went back in the kitchen and Sonia offered the doctor an *empanada*. He waved it away. His stomach had been upset all day.

"A little cup of *manzanilla*?" Sonia offered.

"No no, nothing. This is serious, serious. You have to get him to the city. It will have to be hurried up."

"There is nothing we can do," Sergio said. "It is a matter of currency. The money must be usable."

"Yes, yes, well I've done what I can do."

"We thank you, doctor."

He picked up his bag. "Cannot come back. It is too dangerous."

"Yes, wait. There is a letter he requested to be mailed in the city." Sergio took an envelope out of the cupboard, handed it to Carl." You will read it please."

"No heroics," Carl read. "I am a dead man."

"It cannot be sent."

"No, no, of course." Sergio set fire to it at the kerosene stove and dropped it on the tiles to burn.

"I must leave now." The doctor picked up his bag. "Don't neglect the foot, and watch for signs of insulin shock. Sweating, remember, extreme thirst, weakness. And he must eat."

The captive dozed.

"Perhaps it will be all right, if only he will eat. As long as he is so weak, we can handle the injections and the urine," Sonia said. "You must go now. They must not know you are here. No one must know."

"But if he doesn't eat?" Carl said.

"We will see what happens. If we need you, I will send to the *abasto*."

They went back on the bus. No one had noticed their absence.

CARL DID HIS SHOPPING at the *galeria*, left his baskets at Lino's behind the sacks of rice and lentils. Halfway down the Calle Trece he went up the steps of the Plaza Militar. The yellow bricks were worn below the mortar. Outside the Capilla San Judas he stood and stared into the murmuring dark. A woman passed him, crossed herself and genuflected. He threw away the paper from the *raspado* he had just eaten and went in and stood at the back. A beggar in bare feet walked boldly to the foot of the altar. A boy with his shirttail out swung a brass pot of incense.

"Cordero de Dios," pared the priest, a benighted looking Indian:"...*que quita los pecados del mundo*..."

Should he pray for the *Norteamericano*? He didn't feel worthy. But this felt like the right place.

"Dark smoky chapels," Páez wrote. "Oxidizing our remorse."

Don Rafa, who had just come to the farm from the city for a stay through Christmas, was sitting in front of the Cafe Media Luna with half a bottle of *habanera* in front of him, and a plate of *chicharrones*.

"Not much of a place, Tuxpan, eh? There's a character in a novel by Pío Baroja…I don't suppose you've read Pío Baroja…little novice, about to take her vows. The *Superiora* doesn't like to think of a girl so young giving up the world without a second thought; advises her to walk about the town a bit, think it over. Well, the girl takes a turn around the wretched little place, comes back in half an hour and says it doesn't seem to her such a grand thing, the world. Ah Pío Baroja. *El Último Romántico*. There's a book. I must have read it twenty times. So, you are settled here; you entertain yourselves…?"

"Pretty much," said Carl, thinking of Sergio's opinions about *don* Rafa.

"And what do you do all day?"

"Well, there are the chickens…."

"Ah, the chickens."

"And the pig. And Willi's garden. I've been reading a good deal, the *Doña's* books."

"Ah, so…

"Alejandro Páez. I've been reading his poems in *Las Mañanas*. I even try translating them, just for practice."

"Yes, yes, Páez. I knew him. It was years ago."

"You know him? Is he alive. Might I meet him…?"

"Yes, well I wouldn't wait too long." said *don* Rafa." *Dos cervezas*," he told the waiter, "and A *café tinto*."

"Where is he; do you know?"

"He may be living under some bridge, holding out a bleeding stump and a hat.

"Is that true?"

"Probably not. If it were up to the authorities it would be."

"But why, why?"

"He's old, ill. They found him a place…some friends of mine, journalists, in the old San Juan de Dios Hospital, but a year later the nuns wanted the wing where he was for a residence and asked him to move. He went back to Envigado."

"What is his illness?"

"Diabetes principally. He treats it by taking a syrup made of honey and orange peels. There was a French girl living with him. Someone like you. Came looking for him. But she was not one to handle such a man."

"And does he still write?"

"It is prohibited for any publication of his to pass through the mails or cross a provincial border. There was an anarchist plot two years ago. They blamed an article of his."

The waiter cleared away plates and bottles, put down the two beers and the coffee.

"'*Las tardes asoleadas...*'" Don Rafa raised a finger in the air." 'The sun filled afternoons...Where the sun rules...'

"It was a bullfight he was speaking of. Yes, and Spain, Spain. Iron of Spain. 'Rusted iron of Spain...' oh, our poets! When I was an undergraduate in the school of mines, like you, I tried my hand at a translation. I have my efforts in a notebook somewhere."

Carl thought of the abandoned notebook in the henhouse.

"There was a line I was stuck on. '*La huella de tu luz...*' the 'footprint of your light.' It struck me as wrong, footprint..."

"No, no. It's too heavy," Carl said.

"Exactly. You are exactly right. 'footprint' is too heavy, too quotidian. Perhaps we should collaborate..."

"But you really knew him?" Carl said.

"Oh yes. He ran with our pack of journalists and desperate men during the reign of Olivares Salazar; he used to write his poems on napkins in the Café Carvajal en el Barrio Qnce de Febrero. We were putting out a bi-monthly paper: *O Soledad Bravo*. That was his name for us. Then they took our press, but we printed for a while on the mimeo machines at the University. Then came our brief Republic. A golden age. We brought, out our paper for three, years in a new print shop in the Avenida Victor Hugo, also. His first two volumes of poems. Yes, a golden age. Then the killings began. I left, then, for Tula. And he was exiled to Italy—the gentlemen in the capital being pro-Mussolini. Out of Italy came a long poem, I don't know if it's ever been published. I was studying in Colorado at the time. He was thrown out of Italy by Mussolini; some anti-fascist tracts were traced to him. He would have happily taken credit for them, he told me later, but hey were not his. Nonetheless he came home and was literally under house arrest in the State of Flores.

"I saw him next when I was laying out the route of the railroad Tula-La Florida. We sat in the Hotel Caracas drinking *habanera* to warm the gut, and planning another newspaper; but there were no more newspapers. We married, both of us, the same year. Another of us, Enrique Lazo, was sent as ambassador to Uruguay, and Jairo Menes was made head of his uncle's cement plant. *Es decir*, we became respectable. Yes, that was the last I saw of him. He had four children, I heard, and his wife died in 1954. In 1960, his *Manantiales* was published in Mexico and circulated here secretly. People combed it for conspiracy, but it was the purest lyricism. It was received well in Mexico, and he lived there a while but came back: 'Here is my poetry and my pain,' he said.

"So it is Páez you've discovered, our Páez. I think, sometimes, they take away his writing paper he'll scratch his words in the dust." *Don* Rafa drained his glass. "What is it, what is it, this something in us wants it all recorded somewhere? Yes but where? The germ plasma, I think sometimes, the subatomic particles. You can't trust…you can't trust civilization."

"YOU SHOULD HAVE KEPT your heart," *doña* Berta said to her partner, *doña* Eulalia. The spade would have been good." Eulalia said nothing, but her wattles shook as she paid the kitty. A *sorbete* of *curuba* had been slipped in among the cards and money and the ladies drank it absently.

Blanche concentrated fiercely. She had seen the spade was good, watched the heart fall, making her seven good. After a shocking loss of two hundred *pesos* her first day of play, she'd won eight hundred and seventy some *pesos*, and today she and the young lawyer's wife from Kilómetro Veintisiete were up one rubber. The girl brought plates with cold slices of beef stuffed with vegetables and saffron rice. Room was made on the table. "Have you been married long?" *doña* Eulalia began conversationally to Blanche, while Berta dealt the cards.

"Just a year," Blanche said.

"You must be behaving yourselves very well. This one has been married half the time and look at her…." Eulalia nodded toward the lawyer's wife, four months married and three months pregnant.

"The baby," Berta winked. "Your husband will want…"

"No, he doesn't want," Blanche said, spilling a little rice on her jersey.

"But how can that be?"

"He does not want," she repeated, knowing they were speculating about birth control, a subject in which they were abysmally ignorant.

"You use the aspirin water, then, I suppose," said Berta.

"Aspirin water?"

Blanche was appalled.

"Personally, I find it doesn't work," said *doña* Berta. "I don't let him near me, now, unless I have my period. Last week I woke up and found my nightgown on the floor and him on top of me; I got right up and jumped up and down on the bed. That will get rid of it, sometimes, they say."

The lawyer's wife bid a diamond. "They tell me there's a pill for straightening out the periods; you can get if you go to a doctor and say you're irregular…"

"The Pill, yes," said Blanche. Her partner bid two diamonds. She had four diamonds including a queen, but nothing else in her hand.

"Teresa Villa told me this," said the lawyer's wife, "and the name of a doctor. I could give it to you if you want," she said to Berta.

"Oh, yes, yes. I'm desperate. You won't mention this conversation to *doña* Luz, will you?" Berta said to Blanche.

"No, no." She thought how here you could walk into a drug store and buy whatever you wanted without a prescription. The lawyer's wife raised the diamonds to four. Blanche felt giddy.

"I suppose that's what you use," Berta put to Blanche.

"No. Something else'."

"Ah…"

Blanche was incapable of describing a diaphragm in Spanish.

"Something, something like a bottle top," she stammered.

"In your country are wonderful things," said the lawyer's wife. Blanche laid down her hand.

"If one were to go to the *botica* and ask about this pill, I suppose one might be reported," said Berta. "No, it is better the doctor. You will give me the name perhaps later."

"And if you take this pill, can you still go to church?" asked Eulalia.

"One must try something," said Berta. "One dislikes to sin, but the money doesn't reach, do you see? We are dependent on the *Doña* for the children's school, their dentist. The money doesn't reach. *En fin,* any more *chinitos* and…"

The lawyer's wife finessed Eulalie's spade.

"Olga, you didn't hear this conversation," Berta said to the *muchacha*, who was removing the plates.

"No, *Señora*."

"I say one should accept whatever God gives," said *doña* Eulalia.

"When God gives only three, one can say such things," said Berta.

"I would have had what God gave me," said Eulalia.

Their four hearts was assured.

"Something like a bottle top..." Berta wondered. "Where does it go?"

"Inside," Blanche explained.

"Ah, inside...."

"I would have taken three; I would have taken ten," said Eulalia.

"And your husband a poor accountant like mine," said Berta.

A fig compote was served. "If there's a bit of white cheese you can bring that too," Berta said to Olga. They ate heartily at these afternoons, and often went to bed straight after.

"I'd go on having one after another, too; if I could," said Berta. "Believe it."

They made their bid. Eulalia was quaking with anger.

"Now Eulalia," said Berta. If Eulalia quit the game and went home mad, as had happened before, they would lose their foursome. "I didn't mean my words. You are fortunate in having only three is all I meant to say," Berta soothed, and changed the subject to the Virgin:

"They tell me your Marta's been up to see Her...."

"So she says. Though the girl's a chronic liar," said Eulalia, recovering herself. Blanche dealt.

"Is there really something up there do you think?" asked Berta.

"It's my opinion there is," said Eulalia.

"Magali, the *muchacha* of Elvira down at the *abasto*, has had a miracle," said Olga.

"*Diós!*" exclaimed Berta.

"The intestine of the child continually slipped out...."

"*Virgen santa!*"

"Who told you this?" Eulalia asked Olga.

"Marta."

"Oh *Marta*!"

"But there is something up there!" cried Olga. Magali says it wears an apron of the type they sell in the Casa del Pueblo."

"Someone has possibly rigged it up there," said Berta.

"The *Doña* believes it is a Virgin; and the child *was* cured," Olga stated, and went back to the kitchen.

"I don't know. Maybe she's right. You can't trust Marta," said Eulalia, "But Magali is a good person and the child *was* sick.

"But an apron from the Casa del Pueblo...Someone put it up there, I say," said Berta: "Give people something to talk about."

"An. apron must come from somewhere," said Eulalia. It doesn't bother me."

"You give me two days off, I'll go up and pray for my mother who suffers in the hip, "said Olga from the kitchen door.

"Not possible;" said Berta. "We couldn't possibly spare you this week. Maybe next. If it's still there. I haven't seen it lately. Run, run see if it's still there."

THAT NIGHT, there was a tremor at about three. Carl sat up in bed. It was too cold to get up; Blanche was still asleep on her stomach. It passed, came again. The coffeepot rattled on the stove. The Eternit roof shifted on the guadua poles. Willi came through the curtain separating their rooms, pulling on his pants. "Get out," he shouted over the renewed din.

Blanche sat up. Carl wrapped himself in a blanket, "Come on!" He threw her a poncho hanging over a chair. They stumbled through the jingling kitchen. The soup pot fell off its nail and rolled across the tile. A bottle of *aguardiente* crashed onto the stove and broke. They crossed the drive to the grassy bank under the plantains and sat wrapped in their blankets. The clouds were down heavily and the stable and the big house were invisible. Orlando could be heard pulling out the cow. Then all was quiet, except for the disturbed chickens. Don Rafa walked out of the mist. *Hola.* It will most likely come again. Best stay out here. Not much to worry about. with that Eternit roof of yours. Tiles on the big house more of a worry. Can bury you under a lot of weight. *Upa*, there it comes again."

The sound approached like a locomotive from off to the west where the highway curved off to La Florida, rumbling up from Kilómetro Veinticinco, across the yard, rattling the milk pails in the stable.

"Aye, *Madre*," groaned Orlando's wife from over near the stable. A second tremor was right behind, but this only dislodged pebbles and rocks from the bank below them; they fell in two bounces on to the lower curve of the drive. Carl felt his way toward his panicked chickens. A slab of Eternit roof, it must have been, fell onto the concrete floor of the stable.

"*Madre!*" exclaimed *don* Rafa. A big one this!" Then there was silence again, except for the chickens. Carl had reached them, and discovered all their roosting shelves fallen, but the roof intact. They seemed about to expire from fright. He picked off the boards as quietly as possible, took down one that hadn't fallen yet, but looked likely to.*Don* Rafa came with a flashlight and helped him right the feeding trough.

"Absurd creatures. Not a reasonable bone in them."

It remained still. Carl went through the big house with *don* Rafa. A vase of the *Doña's* had shattered, and a window in the kitchen. Some plaster was down in a bedroom. Nothing major. They brought out some more blankets, a mattress for *doña* Luz and for Berta. "Best stay out from under a roof till morning," said *don* Rafa.

They lay down to sleep. Orlando pulled his kerosene stove into the yard and made coffee. There was another slight tremor just at dawn. Carl woke and sat up. Willi lay sleeping beside him; Blanche, behind. The others were sprawled on the little lawn at the back of the big house. They had dragged mattresses, pillows, blankets, plush animals, water jugs outside. Las Brumas reminded him of some upholstered chair whose stuffing had leaked out, or one of those tenement rooms whose pink flowered wallpaper is revealed to the street by demolition. The *Doña* moved among the sleeping children in a lavender dressing gown under which her pale nightgown hung; her mystery spilled out in this flat morning light.

The cow, tethered to the spigot, waggled her head and mooed softly. Orlando came out of the mist and milked her; then untied her and pushed her into the pasture.

Carl got up. The mist was rising and Miriam and the girl from the kitchen were toasting tortillas over an *ocote* fire. The children moved about. The *Doña* had still not gotten dressed.

Don Rafa was inspecting the stable. A slab of Eternit had fallen into the feed trough, and the forage cutter had tilted off its blocks. Carl helped right it, and they picked up the pails rolling around the floor. Next, they went through the big house. Chinese checkers had fallen off the table and rolled over the verandah. The *Doña's* 15th century oil of *Santa* Teresita of Avila had fallen in the bedroom and come out of its frame. A gutter was fallen into the patio and a great deal of plaster into the kitchen and one bedroom.

The *Doña* brought them coffee and exclaimed over her Teresita, trying to fit the frame back together. "I'll have it fixed in Tuxpan," Carl said, taking the pieces from her. A mild after-shock rumbled underfoot; and they went quickly into the garden, *don* Rafa taking the radio with him. Carl took the picture out of the frame and laid the pieces on a bench. The painting itself was on wood, a hooded woman in dark colors holding a cross in her right hand and a book in her left. The fingers were sausage like and the eyes a bit uneven, but the all over effect was harmonious and grave..

"Mild tremor. 6.4 on the Richter scale," they were saying on the radio. "Epicenter in Palmira, where the historic Hotel Lindberg suffered damage, and a bridge over the Huitenango River was partially destroyed. Minor damage in Tuxpan and Los Chorros." The *Doña* brought them tortillas, wan in her lavender dressing gown, her feet in satin slippers, wet from the grass.

"I used to drink with Filodoro Ochoa in the Hotel Lindberg; it had marble spittoons on every landing," said *don* Rafa.

"So many beautiful things gone, said the *Dona*. "They build again, but it is never the same."

The aftershocks lasted till nearly noon. Carl went in and dressed, then gave the *Doña* her lesson under the fig tree in the front garden. The Teresita was beside them on the bench. "I've always called it my Teresita, but lately I've begun to doubt, I fear she is another saint, Santa Rita," said *doña Luz*, picking up the picture and pointing out what looked like a projectile hole ringed with blood in the forehead. I bought her in an old secondhand shop in Charagua. She had been painted on the door of an old church that had fallen in and been torn down. Someone had sawed her out of the door and painted around her a wreath of leaves in aluminum paint." She lifted the oval mat which was glued loosely over the silver paint to show him. She is very old, I was told by the framer, and quite coated with smoke of candles. He was a man who appeared to know a bit about antiquities and he advised me not to have her cleaned and to cover up the aluminum paint which somebody added centuries later, fortunately only around the border, not touching the saint."

"I have always loved Teresa of Ávila, so I made the mistake of believing this stigmata on the forehead for a bit of damage to the paint."

"And Saint Rita…"

"It is Saint Rita who has the stigmata. If you look closely you can see it is painted. I was deceived by myself…yes."

"You deceived yourself."

"Yes, I deceived myself. But Saint Rita is fine saint. It is just one does not stick to her as soon…"

"Take to her. But why?"

"Well, she had a terrible odor. I am ashamed to think that that should offend me, who cannot even perceive it… It was her punishment for a very…human *falta*."

"Failing," he said. But what?"

"Why she condemned her husband and her son in one moment. Some would say they quite deserved it. She wished them to be dead for their drunken ways."

Carl, who had thought of saints barely at all in his life—they had never been mentioned in his Congregational college—was struck by this and exclaimed, "Well then she must have lived!"

"Of course she lived. Why did you doubt? She was a very ordinary woman with a large, how you say?"

"Burden."

"Yes, burden. She was not like my Teresita who when she was four or five years old tried to run away with her brother to become 'martyrs in Africa,' and was picked up on a dusty road by an uncle who happened to pass in his carriage. It was only after the sin that Rita's sainthood began. She went to a convent and developed the odor, so that no one wanted to be close to her."

"The sin?"

"Of wanting the, the burden, taken off. The husband and the son died within a year of her wish."

"I had no idea," said Carl," that they were such real people."

Later that afternoon, he wrapped the Teresita in brown paper and took the Blue Bus into Tuxpan.

All along the highway, families had dragged armchairs, kitchen tables, kerosene stoves out of the houses and seemed to be playing house in the yards. A bridge was cracked and unusable just beyond Kilómetro Veinte; but, since the river was still low after the dry season, the driver drove down the bank and through the shallow water.

In Tuxpan everything was in the streets; sacks of rice, potatoes, cheap gauze dresses, aluminum pans, salt cod, plastic dishes, plaster saints, plantains, oranges, barber's chairs, reels of lace and embroidery, blue jeans, boots. Lino had made a stall for himself in the central patio of the *galeria*, along with melon and aracacha sellers. Under the vacated arcades, the gutters and many tiles were down, and work was already begun at replacing them. Carl remembered Frank's hurry to patch things up before depression set in. He bought oranges and corn meal and stored them at the lottery sellers near the bus depot.

He took the Saint to a framer and glazier on Calle Septima: A. Bedout and Son. Here, they were sweeping up glass from broken mirrors and framed oleographs, as well as shards of tile. Just as Carl was handing the broken picture over the counter to the young Lebanese, a fresh aftershock came, causing the clerk to leap the counter and run out of the building, leaving Carl holding the picture. He stood a moment, paralyzed, and a bit giddy, feeling an irrational desire to laugh, then followed everyone else into the street. The brick tower of the Capilla de San Bartolomeo swayed giddily for about thirty seconds and it was over.

The young man wouldn't return to the store. It was the old father, finally, who took the frame into a back room, knocked it together and glued it, then cut a new piece of glass and set in a new piece of backing with some rusty galvanized points. As Carl was paying, there was another tremor, but the old man nervously received the money and rang it up.

"I didn't charge the back," he said, hurrying out again to the wooden chair he had dragged into the little plaza and chained to one of the benches.

THEY SLEPT ANOTHER NIGHT out in the damp. No one woke, though Orlando said there was a mild tremor around two. Next morning Carl helped move the card table and chairs out to the garden and the ladies came to play. Consuelo killed one of the hens and cooked an *hervido* with yellow potatoes and yucca. *Don* Luciano came down and stayed to help Orlando replace the section of Eternit in the stable. Up above, he said, they'd suffered the same sort of minor damage: plaster down, windows broken.

Carl wondered about the North American at Sonia's. Was he alive, was he eating? He felt an irrational anger toward him. Wednesday, they'd go. Too often would call attention.

They slept inside that night. The *Doña* went out early with her baskets.

ON WEDNESDAY Seybolt looked thinner. His face was shiny with perspiration." He will not eat," Sergio said.

Carl, Willi, and Blanche

"Sometimes when he wants the aguardiente very badly I can get him to eat a little soup before I let him drink," Sonia said.

"But it is not enough," said Sergio. "I called the doctor; he will send someone from the *Rurales* to put a nose tube."

"Tell him," Sonia said, "he will save himself the tubes if he will eat. You can tell him he will be tied down and very uncomfortable."

"I know, I know," said Seybolt, understanding her. "Let them do what they must. I will not cooperate; but I'm too weak to fight them."

"The money is arranged," Sergio said. "It is only to take him to the meeting place. But it is far and he will not stand the trip as he is. We cannot show them a corpse."

"Why do you do this?" Carl said to the man on the bed. "Your disease can be controlled."

"My disease, yes. Try it yourself. Even at my best, my legs ache so I could scream. I've had this disease nine years—the childhood type, even though it started when I was thirty. That's quite rare. You want to see the muscles in my legs?" He pulled up his pant leg. The thigh muscle was pulled up in a knot, as if no longer attached to the tendon and bone.

"Impotent too; you never knew that, did you, about diabetes? You think it's just a matter of a little insulin. Eyes go, too. I'm blind in my right eye."

"What does he say?" asked Sonia. Carl translated.

"Have you something to drink?" Willi asked.

"*Aguardiente.*"

They brought the lentil soup that Sonia had on the stove, but he shook his head. Sergio gave him some guava juice with the aguardiente in it." It will do him harm in the long run, but maybe in the short..."

"Seybolt drank it. Sergio brought the bottle, poured them all a drink.

"So you do a little 'this and that?'" Seybolt said, wiping his face on the sheet and looking a little revived.

"Yes; we farm a little," Willi said from the windowsill where he was sitting.

"What do you grow?"

"Pepper, beans, corn."

"Have to pee."

They helped him up. He stood weakly, with Willi's help, and urinated into a pail in the corner. Sonia dipped one of the tapes in the urine.

123

Negative. She frowned. There was a slight ketosis. Seybolt started to fall coming back to the bed. Will caught him, helped him zip up his fly.

"They pee like any other *miserable*," said Sergio, "these vice presidents." The afternoon rain had begun. Sonia brought plastic bowls to put under two leaks. A man in a poncho came to the door. Sergio went out in the yard to talk to him, and Seybolt drowsed.

"We have the Jeep," Sergio said to Sonia when he came back in." We start tomorrow. They will send someone this afternoon with the nose tube and the Similac. Tell him this," Sergio said to Carl," And ask him once more if he will eat."

Carl shook Seybolt awake and explained about the nose tube. The man's skin felt loose on his bones, and covered with a film of cold perspiration.

"I will not eat. Give me more *aguardiente*."

They gave him the *aguardiente* in milk this time, and he spat it out.

"Will you stay till it comes?" Sergio asked Carl and Willi.

"Yes, yes, of course," Willi said.

Sonia brought another bottle of *aguardiente* and some limes. "I'm making chicken soup with yucca and potatoes," she said. "You tell him if he will eat it he will avoid a tube." .

Paul Seybolt understood and shook his head. "Give me *aguardiente*," he croaked.

"He is negative," Sergio said. "Perhaps it will avoid the insulin shock." He poured another glass and gave it to Seybolt.

"Four o'clock. They are supposed to be here in half an hour." He paced around the room, sucking limes. Seybolt finished the *aguardiente* and dozed again.

"Dr. Ruiz swore this student he was sending was trustworthy," said Sergio.

"And if he was caught?" Sonia said.

"He has no past...attended a few meetings at the university. They can know nothing of him."

"And if he doesn't come?"

"I'll do it myself," said Sergio.

"We know nothing of inserting nose tubes."

"There's Solita. Perhaps she...?"

"A midwife?"

They waited, drinking Cruz Verde now. Seybolt slept, perspiring in spite of the chill. The rain stopped and the sun shone briefly in through the shutters, then it was dark. They put off eating. "He must be here soon," Sergio said. "Or I will have to go."

A boy of sixteen or so finally came at nearly six-thirty with a nose tube and three cans of Similac.

"And the student? The intern?" Sonia asked.

"He's been arrested."

"But why? Why? He's done nothing…?"

"It will be as an example," said Sergio. "They know whoever has the Gringo will be looking for medical help. The student attended meetings."

"Do you know how to insert the tube?" Sonia asked the boy hopelessly.

"Me, I know nothing. I mop the floors and empty the slops," he said.

Sergio was taking down his poncho from the nail. He would go for the midwife in the next village..

"Go, *mijo*," Sonia said. He is dying. I feel it."

The schoolbooks were pushed to one end of the table, and they sat down in the kitchen and had the soup and fried plantains. "Perhaps it's lucky they arrested him," Sonia said. "They might have let him lead them to us."

"Pig!" Willi jumped up and stood in the bedroom door: "Pig!" he shouted at the sleeping man." You'll let these people be your murderers!"

Seybolt opened his eyes.

"These are good, decent people. They don't want you to die!"

Seybolt wiped his face on the sheet."Give me *aguardiente*."

"No *aguardiente*! Soup. You will drink soup! Bring it!" He gestured to Sonia. She brought a cup of the thick broth.

"Good people, and you will destroy them!" Willi shouted. Sonia handed him the cup. "Drink, now!" He held the cup to the sick man." Drink!"

Seybolt drank and gagged.

"Drink!" Willi yelled. But Seybolt pushed the cup away. "Tube down your nose. You want that?"

Seybolt lay on the bed, weakened and gasping; but shaking his head, "No, no…!" They left him and went back in the kitchen. Our nerves are giving out, Carl thought. He'd better come, he'd better come soon.

"Take him, take him there tonight," Willi burst out.

"Where?"

"The *Rurales*."

"They wouldn't receive him," Sonia said. "They'd turn him away. No, *doña* Solita must come. We must keep calm."

They sat, silent, listening.to the beetles bump against the shutters. A parade of them came in under the door and crossed the room and went out again under the back door. "We built in their path," Sonia said. "Now they come through any way they can or knock themselves dead trying. Every morning I sweep them up."

After they had finished eating," Sonia and the girl washed up the dishes. The boy sat at the; table cleaning the chimneys of the oil lamps. "You should be in bed," Sonia said without her usual conviction, so they stayed up.

"These will be different," Sonia said after a whilc. "These will be a doctor and an engineer."

"Ay, mami, ya no!"

"Yes, the boy a doctor, the girl an engineer. It is decided. They are excellent students. They will have scholarships if God pleases.

"They are each top in their examinations. They will go to the technical school at Los Olmos and to the *Nacional*. Those who finish in the top three at the technical are given full scholarships."

"*Ya basta Mami!*"

"Listen, *don* Carl, listen! You two be quiet; you two have nothing to do with this! If anything happens tomorrow, *don* Carl ...."

"*Que va a pasar, Mami!*"

"The *Doña*, go to the *Doña*. They are innocent children. She will understand that."

"Yes, yes, of course," Carl said.

"My brother's address...here, here! "She pulled a trunk out from under a daybed in the corner of the kitchen, opened it and took out a leatherette box which contained a stack of letters."Here." Taking a blank envelope, she wrote two addresses. "My brother, who lives in Pellicer, and my sister-in-law in the capital. The *Doña* will perhaps see they are sent to one or the other."

"Of course, of course."

"I have told them to run to the cave up there and hide. They know how to get in. They will wait for you there."

"Yes, yes.".

"And that they finish their schooling. A doctor and an engineer. You will remember. The boy, a doctor. He has a compassionate nature..."

"Mami!"

"The girl is more into herself. She will work in a laboratory with her instruments and be happy."

Sergio came back alone at about eight thirty.

"She would not come!" Sonia cried.

"She demonstrated to me its use.

"We can do it."

They sat the gringo up and tied his hands behind his back. Carl sat on his legs and Willi grasped him around the chest. Sergio held the tube up to the light of the oil lamp hung over the bed and blew up a little balloon at the end.

"If he would swallow it, it would be simple; but since he certainly won't, it must inserted through the nose. Miller-Abbot tube," he murmured with satisfaction, applying Vaseline and deflating the bulb at the end. "The little balloon is blown up when the thing is in place and the intestine moves it along. Hold him now."

Paul Seybolt shook his head violently, but Sonia grasped it from the side in her strong arms. Oopa, it's in!" Sergio said, threading it rapidly down, noting the gradations. Then it stopped.

"Not far enough," Sergio frowned. "We haven't reached the intestine. This mark must pass the nostril."

Paul Seybolt had become very calm and still.

Sergio pulled out a length of tube. "He's resisting it."

"What do they do when this happens?" Sonia asked.

"Flouroscopy," Sergio muttered. "But it almost never happens, she told me. He's closing off the gullet. I can feel it." He pulled out the rest of the tube.

"Give him *aguardiente*," Willi said. They held the glass to his lips. He retched, drank again.

"Let him rest a bit. We'll try again." Sergio wiped his face on his sleeve.

"More," Seybolt croaked, and they passed him the bottle. The bucket, he wanted next. Willi brought it. They had to help him stand and urinate. Sonia dipped one of the tapes. "Two plus," she said, comparing it to the chart on the bottle. "Should we give insulin?"

"Better not. The doctor said a little sugar was better than insulin shock." Sergio closed up Seybolt's fly, and remarked again:" Pee like any other Christian, these vice presidents. "Seybolt collapsed on the bed.

"He's very drunk," Sonia said. "I don't like his color. Try again."

They sat him up again. He was almost dead weight this time. The tube went down. "If only we haven't killed him with *aguardiente*." Sonia got the

Similac and attached a funnel to the end of the tube. While Sergio held it up, she poured the gruel in.

"Is it going down?"

"Maybe. I can't tell. It's slow."

"You've made it too thick."

"I followed the directions on the can."

"There, there it goes. He held the tube higher.

"Yes, but slow."

"Something to hold it; I can't much longer," Sergio said.

"The mosquito net, tie it to the…"

That worked well. There was a hook in the ceiling which held a gauze net. Sergio gave the funnel to Carl and found some rubber bands around a doorknob. Taking his belt, he hung the buckle off the hook; then, with the rubber bands, he fastened the funnel to the lower end of the belt.

Sonia stood on a chair to fill the funnel every few minutes or so." It goes faster now," she said. Paul Seybolt was asleep and snoring. The room was poorly lighted, but his color seemed better.

Sergio went into the kitchen and heated the soup. Sonia finished pouring in half of the Similac and they went in to join him. There was a quarter of a bottle of *aguardiente* left. Sergio drank and ate: "Maybe it will come right. Maybe. I thought we were lost. Maybe we are lost. He'll revive. But will we get him to Las Cruces? It's six hours by Jeep. Will there really be a Jeep. If there isn't, it's twenty hours by muleback. He can barely stand to piss."

Sonia got up and went into the bedroom with the Similac.

"He'll have sugar now," Sergio said. "Sugar's better than insulin shock, but unhealthy all the same. Unhealthy."

The boy and the girl were back at their lessons at the end of the table. The girl, her straight coarse hair over her face, was dissecting lines with a compass.

"It makes me itch to 'throw down my shovel and go out there and shoulder a rifle with Chu Teh,'" Willi said, pacing.

"What?" said Carl.

"You won't guess who said that."

"Who?"

"Uncle Joe Stilwell. After Chiang sent him home, Just before the whole Nationalist façade came down to the tune of billions invested. One of these remarks almost got him in trouble with McCarthy."

Carl, Willi, and Blanche

"Who was Chu Teh, Carl asked.

"One of Mao's guys. Uncle Joe was one of my dad's heroes. Used to follow everything he did. A lot of people did. Vinegar Joe. And all that energy for the wrong people. He loved the Chinese soldier though. And he saw how the Communists cared for their own. He went up there and saw them. I don't think he even had permission. Big, healthy guys, trained, cared for. And he saw how Chiang never even noticed things like his people were taxed to death, were starving, soldiers left to die on the field while he worried about a shipment of watermelons. All that energy for the wrong people. Only a few men in history ever had that energy to push troops over mountains, never give up. Simón Bolívar had it. I don't know, maybe some of the ancient guys.

"'Agrarian reformers,' Uncle Joe called them. He loved those guys. Ach, it's all just words. We're no better than Rafael Villegas."

"But what can we do?"

"Nothing. Watch."

"Shall I tell the *Doña?*"

"Why would you?"

"Sonia asked me to have her help the children if anything happens."

"Better wait to see if it's necessary."

When they left for the bus at seven in the morning, the Jeep hadn't come, but there was still a half hour to go. The gringo slept.

IN THE BIG HOUSE they prepared *Nochebuena*. The *Doña* gathered moss, *helechos*, brought out the bark stable, the porcelain holy family—the Child and the Magi left hidden in excelsior until the last. On the day of the *iluminación*, the first of the nine candles was lit and family, servants, the three North Americans gathered before the *Doña's* nativity scene, which took up a whole end of the verandah; a sandy plain with little oases made of real plants and moss.

And each night the *Doña* read one of the nine prayers: "*Bendita eres entre mujeres, Y bendito el fruto…*" while *don* Rafa smoked in the courtyard with *don* Luciano from up the hill, and set off *estrellitas*, little sticks of gunpowder, tossing them in a high arc over the plantains. Eight days, seven days; the porcelain kings began their journey over the mossy plain. The beasts waited, stolid, and Orlando's wife, too, waited heavily on her knees:

"*Bendita eres entre mujeres y bendito el fruto de tu vientre, Jesús.*"

Berta's husband came from the city. He was a quiet man. When the children bothered him he went out to hoe in the garden.

"Another Christmas," *don* Rafa remarked to Carl one day in Tuxpan. How time goes. As Ortega y Gasset said somewhere, 'If life were a toothache that would be an advantage.'

"Carl had finished his grocery shopping and *don* Rafa had replenished his little supply of fireworks, so they walked together to the Café Mil y una Noches. A large man in a white linen suit passed them, standing aside and making a little bow.

"Don Eusebio Alvarez;" said don Rafa, "He lends money at twenty eight percent, lives in a big house out at El Puente, has seven daughters, all beauties. When I pass them on

the street with their mother, I think what a florescence of flesh, what a flowering of hips and bellies."

hey went inside to a table. It would rain any minute.

Don Rafa ordered two glasses of rum.

"Oh, by the way, There are things known about them up there, your friends," he said raising his glass.

"Who?"

"Sergio Molina and his wife. Evidently they are connected with the holding of a wealthy industrialist."

"How did you know!"

"Why in *El Mundo* of course."

"*El Mundo!*" It hadn't occurred to Carl any of the matters he had witnessed those two rainy afternoons up on the mountain could find their way into a newspaper.

But of course it would. Seybolt's kidnapping had been news for weeks before they met him. How could they have been so stupid not to watch the papers! How could they have simply gone back to their chores and expected to one day go up there and find Sonia and Sergio back at their coffee farming and the children at their geometry…!"

"They are among a group of suspects. What do you know for a fact?"

"Well, nothing. Sergio organizes strikes. That's all we know. Your wife also knows that. "Should he perhaps confide in this man, Carl wondered. Could he help? He noted *don* Rafa giving a slow survey of a young woman sitting with a fat *hacendado* at a table nearby and decided not.

"It is said the poor wretch is presumed to be half dead with sugar."

"Who is that? Oh, the industrialist."

"And that he is hidden somewhere around here."

"Of that we heard nothing. Willi likes to go up there and talk about the soil with Sergio."

THE MANGOS RIPENED and the margaritas bloomed extravagantly; the garden in riot after the. rains. Almost obscene, the purple stamen of the plantain.

The sixth night before *Nochebuena* the pregnant child knelt heavily in the candlelight, and Olga from the kitchen sang a barbarous carol from T Chocotán accompanied by the nephews banging pan lids. *Don Rafa* shared a bottle of Cruz Verde with *don* Luciano. They set off two *volcanes*, which sputtered down the hillside into the cane.

A BAT WOKE BLANCHE at four. She heard Orlando's whistle, went out on the stoop.

"*Hola*," he said, coming into the light of the lantern in his kitchen. "What's the matter?"

"There's a bat."

"You want coffee?"

She went and sat on his steps. He came out with two tin cups.

"What's the matter?"

"Nothing. A bat."

"You don't get enough loving maybe?"

"Maybe."

"You tell Orlando about it."

"You're on your rounds."

"I'll just whistle a minute." He blew a blast.

"Why do you whistle? To warn the thieves?"

He laughed. "Vigilantes must whistle. Otherwise their employers might think they are sleeping… Some loving, eh?" He moved closer to her. "Everyone needs some loving."

"I don't believe in sexual intercourse before marriage," she said.

"Never mind. I got more imagination now."

"I could have told you that could get in trouble with those Christian Scientists."

"How I get in trouble?"

"That Mary Baker Eddy, you know she was a transvestite."

"A transvestite. That's, what I like, girls with vocabulary. Always I like to better myself, know cultured women." He put his arm around her, kissed the side of her neck.

"So, you got more imagination now."

"Yeah, Now I would put it in her ear, he, ha." He pulled her to him.

"A sodomist besides." She pulled away.

"Who's that?"

"Mary Baker Eddy."

"You a funny girl." He kissed her again.

"And your rounds?"

"You wait. I go?"

"No."

"Come with me then."

"All right."

At the top of the pasture he blew a blast on his whistle, and then spread his poncho under one of the silkcotton trees that marked the division between the *Doña's* property and the *Franceses*. She sat down on it and pulled her own poncho around her. He sat next to her and traced a finger along her jaw.

"Funny girl."

"It's cold."

"I warm you. Tell me something."

"What?"

"You sleep with him too?"

"Who?"

"The other one."

"Willi? No."

"Why not?"

"Willi's funny."

"How, funny?"

"He doesn't want to spoil things."

"How spoil?"

"Between him and Carl. Willi's the only one of us knows what he's doing here. Funny, us talking English."

"I love the English. I go back there so quick I have a chance. You take me, eh?"

"We aren't going back."

"Yes, you will go. No one stays here. You take me, eh? You take me with you?"

"It's crazy. You all want to go there."

"Sure we would go! All of us would go, every miserable son of a *puta*, every *alacrán*, every *cucaracha*;" he said."Here there is nothing. *Nada, nada! La sopa de la nada.*"

"What's that?"

"That is nothing soup. 'What is for soup tonight?' say my father . '*Nada,*' say my mother. '*La sopa de la nada.*' It is old joke."

"Listen, I go back so quick…"

"But you're married," Blanche said.

"That is the *Doña*. That is no matter."

"You could take her with you, Miriam?"

"Her, no. She belong here. I send her something. Here, sit closer; take this off here."

He pulled off her poncho and her sweater, and lay beside her, his leg astride her legs. "Beautiful, beautiful. *Don* Carl, I bet he don't appreciate you."

"He did once. He was happy enough to get me."

"How he get you?"

"I was engaged to his cousin. He went overseas…"

"Yes, yes," he pulled up her nightgown and pinched her breasts.

"He was killed in the war."

"You love him, the cousin?"

 She thought of John a minute. "Yes."

"And him, *don* Carl?"

"It's *her* he loves, you know."

"Who?" he undid his pants.

"The old woman."

"The *Doña?*"

"Yes."

133

Orlando was shocked. "But she wouldn't ever…"

"Of course not. It's impossible. That's why he likes it. It's mental love. Some kind of mental…"

"Like the Christian Scientists, ha ha!" He got up: "I'll just whistle…"

"Hurry. It's cold."

"Hurry, she says, the little woman. Yes yes, I hurry." He blew a blast and crawled back to the blanket: "He is coming, your Qrlando, coming. There, there, I put it where it belongs, yes?"

"Yes, yes, hurry!"

"Unless you prefer it in your ear?"

"Idiot!"

"Ah, *la mujercita, la palomita…!*"

IN ORDER TO CALL LESS ATTENTION to their absence, Willi went alone up the mountain to see what had happened. He found the children at the outdoor table with their homework, and Sonia among the drying coffee beans. The Jeep had not come, but *El Vicepresidente* was still alive. Sergio had got the knack of the nose tube. It was worrisome, yes, that their district and some of their associates were being named in the papers.

"But we go on, *don* Willi," said Sonia. "We have a crop ready to sell, as you see," she indicated the burlap drop cloths covered with ripe coffee beans spread all about her.

Willi told her about *don* Rafa's suspicions.

"Oh, he will never harm us; but it is best to keep from him what we can. We will be discreet. Don't come again unless I send for you."

"But how will we know?" Willi asked.

"There are the newspapers."

"No, we will come, one of us, when we can."

"All right. You are very good to us. The *Doña* will help if there is need. I have given directions to *don* Carl. The children…"

THE MORNING OF NOCHEBUENA, the *carnicero* came to the farm up the hill to kill the pig. Carl heard the squeals at five in the morning; he got up and pulled on his pants and shirt. Willi was up already in the kitchen.

"Hurry," he said, "I want to see all of this." He gave Carl a tin mug of coffee, and they climbed the hill behind the stable.

Clouds covered the slopes, rolling through the coffee bushes and eucalyptus trees. They climbed through the wire fence and up a slippery path, catching at the clumps of *argentina* grass. The sun was just behind the *cordillera*; thin rays broke through the pile of purple clouds which would bring the day's storm. Tijeretas rose and fell in front of them. At the top of the field they climbed through another double strand of wire and were on the dirt track from Kilometro Veintisiete, which curved to the right and climbed up to the stone steps below *Los Frances* stucco and brick bungalow. They entered the patio, where at a long table covered with oilcloth *doña* Eulalia, her two servants, Marta and Lidia, and their own Olga and Miriam sat chopping messes of cilantro, parsley and green onions.

Out behind the house, Luciano and the *carnicero* stood in the stable, waiting for the blood of the drawn pig to collect in an aluminum washtub. Just outside, Orlando had built a fire with an improvised spit from which two large kettles were hung. When the bleeding was completed, the carcass was skinned and the head cut off and thrown in the boiling water. The steaming intestines were pulled out and washed under the spigot. *Dona* Eulalia brought out the wooden bowls full of chopped herbs and onions and dumped them into the congealing blood in the aluminum tub. This mixture was then ladled into the tied off gut to make blood sausage. These were boiled in the pot with the head. Next the fatback was removed and sent into the kitchen to be fried for breakfast. Eight o'clock by now, the clouds were lifting. Glittering droplets condensed on the plantains and coffee bushes. Carl and Willi fed the fire with ocote sticks and deadwood from under the trees. *Doña* Luz arrived; Olga brought out *chicharrones* and hot chocolate, and they sat away from the smoke on milking stools to eat.

The *carnicero* went to work then, stretching the carcass on a platform of rough boards. He hacked off the trotters, which went into the pot, then cut off the two haunches. Eulalia had a huge wooden vat filled with salt water and nitrate ready to receive these, a heavy stone to weigh them down, and a tight fitting lid to keep out the dogs. The loins, with the bone removed, were stretched out in long wooden troughs and covered with the same onions and cilantro that had gone into the sausage; then a mixture of beer and orange juice was poured over them. "These will go in the oven tonight," Eulalia explained to Willi, who was copying down the recipes in a notebook.

The day's storm darkened the sky. The table where the herb choppers sat was moved under a roof at the far end of the patio. The purple clouds piled up and the wind rose, rattling the plantain leaves. Luciano rigged a tarpaulin over the fire and the woodpile. The sausages were fished out, and Olga carried some of them off to fry in the kitchen. The rest were looped from the rafters. The salivating dogs hung about and were thrown bits of gristle and bone which they carried off into the coffee bushes. Thunder rolled; it grew dark, and fat raindrops pattered on the zinc roof of the stable. A child dressed as a pirate ran out of the house:

"Está servido."

They left the fire to the *carnicero*, who was served a plate of food outside, and went in to sit at the long table at the end of the patio. Olga and Miriam brought plates of *chicharrones*, sausages, fried plantains, saffron rice, peppers in vinegar. Rain poured off the tiles into the philodendrons and rubber trees. "Eat up," said *don* Jorge. "It will have to last you till midnight."

The great bruised clouds raced overhead; suddenly a white sun broke through. The patter slowed; the drains gurgled. An almond *turrón* was brought and sliced with little cups of black coffee. Miriam, looking wan, cleared the table. Eulalia went to baste the meat. *Don* Rafa took aguardiente to the *carnicero*; and *don* Jorge offered Will and Carl cigars.

"What a lot of work," *don* Jorge said, stretching out in a hammock. "My wife gives herself this trouble twice a year. There're plenty of beds, anyone wants a nap."

A series of dark bedrooms opened off the patio. Carl found a small room with an iron bedstead. Two army blankets were folded at the bottom of the bed. He wrapped himself in one of these and fell into the deep sleep that the heavy blankets seemed to induce. In another room, Eulalia's daughter slept beside her suckling child. *Don* Rafa slept on an army cot and *doña* Luz on Eulalia's big iron bed. The *carnicero* dozed on a bench in the stable. He had been up since two in the morning.

CARL, WAKING IN THE DARK ROOM felt stupefied with food and sleep. He went to the spigot and washed his face. Work had begun again. The gelatinous liquid in the kettles was poured through a strainer into five long tin molds; then, what was left behind in the strainer was picked through and the bones thrown to the dogs. The rest: brains, tongue, trotters, bits of bristle become tender with long cooking, meat from the front quarters were chopped fine and stirred into the gelatin. The dying fire was built up again, and one of the hindquarters spitted to roast. The *carnicero* had gone, taking with him a side of fatback, his payment. Luciano tended the meat, basting it with *habanera*, which caused the flames to leap. *Don* Rafa had brought out a bottle of *aguardiente*.

"Gives herself this trouble when we could have stuck it all in a freezer down in the city," said *don* Jorge.

"Used to keep it all salted before the hydroelectric. Didn't taste like much," said *don* Rafa. Smelled to heaven by the time we ate the last of it. *Don* Luciano here would remember. You remember how we used to keep meat before the hydroelectric?"

"Yes. My father would smoke it."

"How long would it keep?" Willi asked. "Weeks? Months?"

"More like weeks."

"Troublesome beasts," said don Jorge. "We'll have to take half of it down to the city day after tomorrow, in any case. Up around Kilometro Cincuenta you can keep meat without refrigeration, not here."

"I remember I was living in the capital, one of my clerks brought me a pig up the elevator, presented it to me for *Nochebuena*," said *don* Rafa. I had to give half of it to the swindler at the butcher's in order to get it taken care of.".

"One thing you can say for up here in the mountains, the *carnecero* takes his side of fatback and a bottle of Cruz Verde and considers himself well paid," said *don* Jorge.

Don Rafa moved out of the range of the smoke. The nephews and two of Eulalia's grandchildren had dressed themselves up as pirates and cowboys and were throwing *estrellitas* into the coffee bushes. The sun dropped behind the *cordillera*, and some rockets from Kilómetro Veinticinco burst among the eucalyptus trees. Berta came up the hill with the rest of the children. Orlando and *don* Alberto made several trips bringing gifts, salads, a kettle of bread soup, two roasted chickens done in Orlando's oven, a bucket of *tamales*.

Don Rafa opened a bottle of' Cruz Verde and sliced up a green mango. He and *don* Jorge had begun their serious drinking and didn't touch the bits of Genoa sausage and white cheese, the cups of bread soup with sherry that were sent around. The children seemed drunk to Carl, reeling about as harlequins, Cinderellas, pirates. But he realized it must be a phenomenon of his own drunkenness. The little girls tripped on the hems of their long dresses: "Papa, give us *estrellitas*."

"Papa. When does *el Niño* come?" asked the smallest child.

At midnight, *mijo*," said his father, who was hoeing calmly in *don* Jorge's garden. Carl took some soup and closed his eyes to steady the world.

"COME," ORLANDO SAID to Blanche, pulling her into the trees. "There's no one below."

They slipped and slid down the hillside. He had a bottle of *habanera* with him, which he passed her. "My girl," he said, slipping his hand under her poncho and into her shirt. "No one care if I whistle tonight, eh?" He pinched her breast. She drank the rum, shivering:

"It's cold."

"Warm in my place," he said. "Oven's been on all day."

"Not there."

"Yes, in the bed." They felt their way around behind the stable and through the plantain grove. He lit a match. "Come quick!" He found the lantern and lit it, bringing it into the kitchen and setting it on the floor.

"No, no light," she said.

"Yes, yes, to see you." He unwrapped her poncho, started on her buttons. Her bowels felt watery, as if she had the dysentery coming on again. He took off her shirt. "This now;" he

undid the waist of her jeans, pulled them down and ran his hands over her belly: "Yes, yes, beautiful, beautiful."

"Sick," she murmured and ran out to the porch and vomited into the vines. He came out behind her, held her from behind. "OH, Christ, oh, Christ, I hate being sick! Go away, go away!"

"It will pass, it will pass. *Ahora sí, ahora sí.*" He held her. She hung over retching, retching; then she had to run to the latrine. He followed her with the lantern, stood over her while her bowels turned to water. "Now, now, it passes," leading her back to the bedroom. "Better now, better now, yes."

She lay across the bed. He rubbed her, kissed her all over. "I have you here. I have you in all the beds, in the *Doña's*..."

"Oh, no! God! Oh God!" She felt better.

"A little drink, just a little." He passed her the bottle, "Just a sip, easy." She drank, coughed. He slipped off his clothes, lay beside her, stroked her pale, inner arms: *"Tan blanca que es, doña Blanca,"* he repeated as he lay across her.

"WE MUST GO UP. I have a bad feeling," Carl said.

"Later. When they begin the firecrackers, and the women are praying. It won't be noticed that we're gone," Willi said.

Bursts of red and green rose over Kilometro Treinta." Big doings in Kilometro Treinta tonight," said *don* Jorge, "Luz Marina Rosano was named Queen of the Sugarcane."

"The girl from Zacapa?"

"She was born in Tuxpan. It was on the radio they've turned over the Brigadier's Jeep and there's been a stabbing."

"*Cielos!*"

"A character in a *cantina* said she had silicone breasts."

"*Que barbaridad!*"

Another burst from below. Luciano came from the wood where he had gone for more kindling.

"A nice face, this meat," said *don* Jorge. He poured some *habanera* over it.

"What a thing to say about one of our women. Silicone, breasts!"

Olga sent word from the kitchen that the pregnant child had stomach cramps.

"Probably too much turrón," said Berta; she told Olga to have her lie down. "Her time isn't for three weeks yet." She wiped soot from the face of her youngest.

"Is the *Niño* coming?" he asked his mother.

"Not for another couple hours."

"Where is Orlando?" asked *doña* Luz

"He's taken himself off somewhere. Probably Kilometro Treinta."

"*Now* is the *Niño* coming?"

"But *mijo*, it's only two minutes since you asked," said Berta. "Do you know your piece? Say your piece for me."

"*Mambru se fue a la guerra*

Que dolor, que dolor, que pena.

Mambru se fue a la guerra.

No se si volverá…"

the child shouted, and ran away.

"At eleven thirty the younger children were sent to try to bring the men inside without success.

"…used to bottle it in the same bottle as their impotable alcohol back in '46," *don* Rafa. was saying to Luciano. "Same green cross on the label." He brandished the bottle of Cruz Verde he was holding. "I remember we kept it all on a shelf in the kitchen over the sink. One October we were up here shooting *perdices* with the old man and my cousin Alfonso; and Lucita takes down the wrong bottle, brings it in on a tray with glasses and all. Well, Alfonso and the old man toss it off the way you do with *aguardiente*, follow it with a couple limes. I'm about to do the same when I see Alfonso clutch his gut. 'I'm a dead man,' he croaks, goes to lay himself out in the hammock and sings himself a requiem from beginning to end. *Carajo!* The two of them waiting to die. I'll never forget…"

One of the children was tugging at his sleeve and telling him they must come in.

"Not now, *hijo*. We still have the big rockets to throw."

"…the old man just sat in the chair like an idol. Not a word, now and then a belch. Oh, he had a gut of lead the old man."

"It is quarter to twelve. We must pray without them," said *doña* Luz, leading the children and servants into the verandah.

"But the rockets…," said the nephews.

"The *Niño* cannot come until we pray," said Berta, pushing the children into the room.

Carl stood with *don* Alberto in the dark entryway, uncertainly hovering, the two of them, between men's affairs and women's. The *Doña* read the prayers for the last day. One exhausted child lay in her lap; two more clung to their mother. The older children knelt in the front, their faces on a level with Eulalia's rustic stable and its porcelain figures. Behind stood the servants, their faces lit by the flickering candles. The pregnant child crouched off to one side, clutching her belly.

The *Doña* finished her reading, and Berta's heavy voice began the *Salve Maria's*, rising and falling monotonously. A rocket went off, and another in the distance. Carl looked at the *Doña*, who was looking intently at the manger waiting for the Child. He thought of a line from Henry Adams:

In the Virgin of Dreux, the mother is said to be absorbed in the child, as the surrounding windows all contain her enemies.

Miriam groaned and the *Doña* went to her and led her from the room. He wondered where Blanche was. He supposed she might be asleep in one of the bedrooms.

"*La torre está en guardia*

La torre está en guardia.
Quien la destruirá?"

The boys sang. And the girls:

"*Iré a quejarme*
Iré a quejarme
Al gran Rey de Borbón!"

Don Alberto looked at his watch. "Midnight," he said.

"*El Niño!*" the children shouted. Eulalia, feeling under the skirts of the table, brought out the porcelain figure, which she gave her oldest granddaughter to place in the straw.

The children, revived from their stupor, tore at the wrappings of the gifts, which. were passed out by Berta and Eulalia. Calmly, calmly!" scolded *doña* Luz, but she was ignored.

The haunch was brought in, and saffron rice, baked plantains, roast chicken, fried yucca, *tamales* wrapped in banana leaves, fruit salad. The children, revived by their toys, paid little attention to food, and *don* Rafa and *don* Jorge still refused to come in.

"NO ONE WILL KNOW."

Orlando put the lantern down on the floor of the big bedroom. Blanche stood in the doorway, saw herself from the waist up in the big mirror above the dressing table.

"Come." He lay on his back on the *Doña's* bed, waiting. "They are all up there above. How can they know we are here?"

"Why must we?" she said. "Why must we in this room?"

"Because you're my lady," he said." My *doña* Blanca. Come." He held out the bottle.

She drank.

"Lie down here by me."

"No." She held the blanket around her.

"I told you. They are all up there. The men are drunk and the women are praying. "Turn

out the light then."

"There, there." He turned down the wick. She went to him. I am lost, she thought, now I am lost.

MIRIAM WAS DISCOVERED bent over the kitchen sink. *Diós Santo! Where is Orlando?"* cried Berta. He was discovered coming up the hill and sent to take the girl home and fetch Solita.

Carl found Blanche alone on the dark verandah. "What's the matter?"

"Nothing."

"Don't you want to eat?"

"I…"

"What is it?"

"Something awful."

"What?"

"Something awful's happening."

"To you?"

"To us."

"Where've you been?"

"Around. I went to lie down."

"Are you sick?"

"Yes."

IT WAS THREE IN THE MORNING when they went down the mountain. Orlando was gone off on his bicycle. The girl moaned softly in the back room of the hut. The children were carried off to bed. Luciano and *don* Rafa smoked in the courtyard, finishing off a bottle of Cruz Verde. Carl sat on the stoop. Blanche had gone to bed. Willi came in and put on fresh clothes. "I'm going up."

"Go, Yes, go! Shall I come?"

Blanche coughed and gagged in the back room.

"No. She'll notice if we're both gone."

WILLI STOOD IN THE DOORWAY of the cottage. There were no signs of Christmas here. Sonia sat at the table, and he could see through the doorway that the Similac bottle still hung from the hook that held the mosquito net.

"Nothing," said Sonia. We do not hear. We had a message two days ago they were to come this morning with a Jeep. We have waited all day."

"Not even a message?"

Carl, Willi, and Blanche

"Nothing. Sit. Have some coffee. Sergio sleeps for an hour. I am watching." Sonia spoke the mixture of basic English and Spanish with which she communicated with Willi.

Willi took coffee from the stove. There seemed to be an increased army of beetles passing across the kitchen floor.

"The *temblor* weakened some of the foundation, so now they find their way through the house as much as they want."

"Why do you think the Jeep doesn't come?"

"Something has happened. *Don* Willi, Sergio and I will go with the *Americano* if the Jeep comes. But the children will not go. They are to run to the cave until whatever is to happen will be. Then they will go to Solita and she will send word to you. The *Doña* must come for them. I have given instructions to *don* Carl.

"They are to go to my brother. He has the address. They are to study and receive scholarships. The boy is to be a doctor, and the girl an engineer. She must be firm in this, for they do not listen to me…. They are too young."

Willi frowned. He could think of nothing to say.

"Perhaps it is not necessary. You can wait a week. If we do not return, a message will be sent."

"I will take them now. Let me take them now."

"No, they would not go. They are serious children, and good. We must respect their wishes in this. They will hide when the Jeep comes and then run to Solita."

"You should come now, with them. Let Sergio go!"

"I cannot, *don* Willi. You know what I am. What we are."

"Tell me then. If we have no word, and you are gone. Who then?"

"Who?"

"Who then I go to?" Willi reverted to pidgin speech when he talked to Sonia.

"I tell you that and you become too involved. Now you are simply our friend. You talk to Sergio about the soil. The coffee crop. I tell you more, you are in danger like us."

"Tell me more."

"Aye, *don* Willi!"

"Tell me more."

"The pharmacist at Kilometro Treinta.. Talk to him."

"QUE NO AGUANTOOOOO!" groaned the girl

"So it begins, does it," said *don* Rafa.

"Will it be long?" Willi asked. He had gotten a lift back down the mountain with a trucker and decided not to bother going to bed.

"Could be, the first. Could be a day or more."

"Nooooooooo! *Que me mata!*"

"*Aguanta, hija.*" said *don* Rafa."It's only the beginning. It's only the beginning."

"Is there anything we can do for her?" Willi asked.

"Nothing, nothing. It takes its course. You never had a child? Never had a woman who had a child?"

"Never," said Willi. There are no children in my family."

"There are always children, I am thinking….".

"Not in my family. I am the last. I will be the last," Willi said.

"Ay, *ay!*"

"A strong girl. Hear her yell," said don Rafa. The last eh? A pity. It will make your mother unhappy."

'Yes; she's on the side of ongoing, my mother...all mothers."

"And you aren't?" *don* Rafa passed the bottle. "How is that?"

"Somewhere there has to be an end. Someone to take it all and force it into some kind of shape…"

"Ah…"

"…make some kind of statement."

"Poetry, I used to think…," said don Rafa. What is it, I wonder, this something in us wants it all recorded somewhere?"

He walked outside of the circle of lamplight. The girl was moving about. Something fell over in the cottage. "I'll take her some rum," said *don* Rafa, going in with the bottle.

It became quiet, and Willi fell asleep for a time in a hammock.

NEARLY DAWN. The mist rose in tatters. The girl was screaming; Orlando still not returned. Carl sat on the porch holding his head. Don Rafa came out in slippers.

"The old woman will be with another," he said." Ah, well, it's better without her, I've always felt. I never liked Solita with her injections, putting the infant to sleep, so it forgets to breathe. Olga is up; she will go over."

Carl, Willi, and Blanche

Something heavy fell over in the hut; the girl shuffled from room to room, bumping into the furniture.

"Mongrel bitch I had once," said don Rafa,"…ran in circles, dropping her litter here and there. Red as a fox. Dropped one of her whelps in my shoe, another under the porch. Dead, both of them, when we found them."

"*Nooooo!*" the girl bellowed," *Ni un momento mas!*"

"*Aguanta pues, si no hay remedio,*" said *don* Rafa."In my day they delivered themselves hanging from a rope tied to the rafters. In hammocks too; that was a trick. Woman I knew, once, dropped hers in the river while she washed clothes. No, better without Solita and her ampules. I'm not the only man to say it. It doesn't do to ask the women. You don't ask a woman to be objective."

"*Uy, uy, uy.*"

Something else fell over and broke. Willi woke and got out of the hammock. He went to the spigot and ran some cold water over his face. The patio was filled with a silvery half-light. Clouds were massing off to the west.

"No, no, no NO!"

He found a bottle of Ron Viejo and took it over to the other cottage. The girl was crouched in a corner of the kitchen, her eyes wild.

"Have this," he said, holding out the bottle, "*Tenga.*"

She wouldn't get up. He found a glass on the floor, filled it and took it to her. She drank it, choked. He gave her more. She drank it, then settled in a heap, moaning. "I'll stay with you, shall I?" Willi said, righting a chair and sitting down. She stared at him. He was speaking English without thinking. Then she began screaming: "No, no, no!"

"You want me to leave?"

She got up and began running again, stumbling over the debris on the floor. He backed out: "I'll get Olga," he said. "You must have someone. Yes, I'll get Olga…"

Olga came out, and The *Doña*, with armfuls of linen. "It won't be yet," Olga said after she had settled the girl in bed. "The child is high in the womb. She is frightened is all. She is young."

Don Rafa threw his cigarette down the hill: "Aye, these girls, these girls! There was one once, working in the kitchen, a little brown thing with many pigtails. She had never seen a light bulb, thought a garden hose would produce water wherever you took it; she was going to take one in a suitcase to her old mother in the Tlocotan who had no water. *Ay Diós!*"

"There he is!" Will cried.

A pale bicycle light wavered below on the road, turned the corner and came slowly up. Orlando walked the bicycle, a figure beside him, wrapped in a blanket. They came into the courtyard, which was now filled with pale sunlight.

"She was with someone else," Orlando said.

Solita was an ageless Indian with a gray blanket thrown over her shoulders, and over that a purple shawl. She carried a worn briefcase. Orlando led her into the hut. *Basta*," she said to the moaning girl; "You be quiet." Her dark figure moved about in front of the lamp.

"She'll give her an injection," *don* Rafa said. "She'll settle her."

Willi made coffee. They sat at the table on the porch as the sky lightened. *Don* Rafa perused Tuesday's *El Nacional* that lay on a chair. "Look at this, another of our homemade buses fallen off the road into a ravine. Sixty people dead. One of these new aircraft, a Boeing Constellation, you'd think. Sixty farmers, some chickens, a pig no doubt, cadaver in a tin box…"

Orlando came out of the hut and sat on the stoop. "It'll be hours," she says.

"*Sí, hombre*. What kept you?"

"She was with a woman in La Florida. There was a hemorrhage."

"Women," said don Rafa. Always something faulty with the plumbing. I have one *volcán* left. We'll set it off when your son is born."

"Yes, man!"

"Right off the cliff there, over Kilometro Veinticinco." Don Rafa walked over to the edge of the courtyard and set up the little rocket. "For the little president, eh? That's why Orlando came back to this country of the very devil. So his son can be native born, eligible for the presidency, eh?"

"Oh sure!" said Orlando.

"Come," *don* Rafa called them. "You'll see the sun clear the cordillera." It was an unusually clear day, in spite of the massed clouds. The raw red gash where the Carretera al Mar rose above Kilóometro Veinticinco was visible through a break in the mist; and off to the east, the diminutive Barrancas-La Florida train could be seen following the wide curve of the Rio Chepa.

"It was Enrique Wolfe and I laid that rail," said don Rafa. Narrow gauge. Fool thing. They have to transfer the cargo into standard cars when they cross the line into Chorritos.

"*Uy!*" moaned the girl, "*Uy!*"

"*Te callas, te callas, oye*," from Solita, but not unkindly.

Carl, Willi, and Blanche

"Have their ways of killing here, too," Blanche murmured behind Carl in the doorway, where she sat.

"In Loma Alta they've abandoned the whole railway system," said *don* Rafa, returning to the porch and lighting another cigarette. "They have the new railway the length of the state. Of course, in Loma Alta they have the commercial instinct. We're farmers here compared to them. Peasants. Who, here, has ever made money on anything but cattle, rice, or real estate. Only business men here are the Arabs."

"I never have been able to stomach the Arabs," said Orlando.

"Not a place for us, Carl. It's death. I feel it."

"Uy! Uy! Uy!"

"You told her to give her a sedative?" *don* Rafa asked Orlando..

"Solita doesn't let them scream for long."

"They have it, though, the commercial faculty, these *Turkos*. You have to admit. Oh, they'll never have souls like us if they live here a thousand years."

"Carl, you hear me, Carl!"

"Of course, next to your Gringo, there's nothing like your German for commercial faculty. You can have your Arab. What do they do but hang their stuffs from the awning and sleep in their doorways…? You take *Herr* Luker who ran the mine at Aramburu. When I was twenty, I had a project of studying the commercial faculty in *Herr* Luker.

"Luker used to come into the *cantina* and drink on anisette, never talk to anyone. Just drink up, then slap a coin on the counter and leave. I used to admire him doing that. We talk, we Latins, we talk too much. Our *voluntad* flows out of us in talk…Well, I was twenty. This Luker had a pair of Hungarian boots I admired. I used to think if I had a pair of boots like that…*caramba*, the things one thinks of when one is twenty!"

"Fucking talk!"

"The devil's own country, eh? Place where Judas lost his boots.".

"Fucking…!"

Don Rafa turned around to look at her: "*Pero, doña* Blanche…".

"Fuck you, fuck you all, fuck you all!" Carl grabbed her, held her from behind"

"Fucking, fucking, fucking, fucking …!"

"She is hysterical. It has been too much. We will go in," said *don* Rafa. "We will go to bed; there is nothing we can do out here."

Solita was sent over to give Blanche an injection. She slept and woke, slept and woke. Dreamed of Belle, of a small monkey being born to Belle.

They got up at noon. It was quiet. Willi found *don* Rafa smoking in the garden. "How goes it?"

"Labor stopped. Solita is letting her rest. Later, she will give quinine to start it again."

"All over again?"

"Yes. A dangerous thing, a dangerous thing."

The ladies came to play hearts and eat *turrón*, but Blanche didn't go over.

She was curled up on her the big iron bed they shared, moaning. At times her moans repeated the timbre and rhythm of the moans that came from the cottage next door; for the quinine had been administered and labor had resumed. Carl sat at the foot of the bed trying to read. He wanted to touch Blanche, but she wouldn't let him.

Willi hoed in the beans, to put to some use the restlessness in his muscles that wanted to take him up the mountain. *Don* Rafa had brought the radio out to the stable and was listening to it as he wrote up the records of the hen's laying. Willi kept an ear out, but could only pick up scraps of a *novela*. He was afraid of seeming to listen. The moans rose and fell, but the exhaustion of the previous night, the repetition of something already lived, took the urgency out of them.

AT EIGHT THAT EVENING, the child, a boy, was born dead.

"So," said *don* Rafa, coming out from the big house to where they sat on the stoop." *El Presidentito* is dead. The little President is dead...

"Colleague of mine, I remember, went to study mining engineering in your esteemed country, married, there, a young compatriot of yours, made her pregnant and brought her back here to have a child.... Native born, he wanted the child to be, eligible for president...

"Well, she had a terrible time. Child was born dead, like this one, in spite of being born in a city hospital. When we heard about it, we said what a pity. A little President was dead..." "This one in there," he shrugged a shoulder toward Orlando's hut." This one might have been a little president...little brown president to promise holidays to the workers, yes...

"*Pero está muerto. El Presidentito está muerto.*"

Carl went in to Blanche. She was up and dressed. "I'm leaving," she said. She had on her Boston Common T shirt.

Chapter 4

It was on the radio. The holders of the kidnapped executive had been taken in.

"A Jeep was sent and they were all taken to the capital," *don* Rafa told Willi.

"Yes, Willi said in anguish.

"They were expecting it to take them to to Purua," he confessed to *don* Rafa. What

was the good of concealing things from him any longer?

"Oh God! Oh, God! I can't believe...We thought everything would be all right. How, how?"

"A Jeep was sent; but it was sabotaged. Someone had talked. Two government agents were along."

"And are they killed? Sonia ...!"

"Sergio's in prison. The woman and children I don't know. Arms were found..."

"Yes, yes, there were guns. We saw them."

"You were very foolish to go there."

"They were good people."

"I imagine they were."

"Did the man die? The American."

"He is said to be near death."

"Oh, God! It wasn't them. Himself, he killed himself. They tried to save him."

"A bad diabetic, the papers say."

"Yes. He refused to eat. They sent to the Rurales for a doctor after they had trouble getting him to eat. No one would come. They sent a boy with a nose tube, Similac. Sergio put the tube in himself. No one would help. They were left to themselves."

"And you?"

"We couldn't do anything. We were supposed to talk him into wanting to live. His mind was made up. His wife had left him. His son was some kind of misfit. I guess we reminded him of the son. We were worse than useless. And he was already very ill. Going blind. Impotent."

"An unhappy event all around. This Sergio will be shot; and others too, whether they helped or not. There will be examples made. It won't do their cause much harm. They're purposely decentralized. That's probably why no one would help. Unhappy, yes, unhappy."

"The children...I promised Sonia, the children! They were to hide where the arms…"

"They found the arms. They won't be there. You won't find them. This is a more serious matter than you appear to realize. Arms were found. A North American is dead, or almost."

BUT THEY WENT. They had to see. They had to wait three days as the rains were so hard and steady the road washed out and it was almost impossible to walk around in it without being practically drowned."White+- rain," they called it.

When they got there, they found no one, and the house was burned.

They walked around it, kicking in the ashes. Evidently it had been torched at the side where the bedrooms were. That part was fallen in; but the fire had burned out, leaving the kitchen intact. There were the two mattresses still on the floor, and the pot of soup and kettle of coffee on the kerosene stove. The children's books and papers were still at the end of the table where the girl had sat; and the two oil lamps the boy had been cleaning.

They climbed the hill at the back. The boards with the branches stapled to them were thrown about, and the crates pulled out and overturned. Books and weapons were gone. Gorky's *La Madre* lay face down in the mud. Carl put it in his pocket. A dirty child watched them.

"Did they take all of them," Carl asked.

"Sí, en un Jeep."

BLANCHE WAS ON THE STEPS with the backpacks. She and Orlando were going as far as Tuxpan in the car with *don* Alberto, then on to the capital in *por puesto*. A priest had come, was inside the hut with the *Doña*, praying. Orlando was in the plantain grove hammering together a box of *palo santo*.

"I can understand she is upset, *doña* Blanche. It is understandable, yes." said *don* Rafa. He held out a hand: "I have enjoyed our conversations."

Blanche extended a limp hand.

"You will take *por puesto* from Tuxpan?"

"Yes, to the capital."

"Perhaps you'll come back some day?"

"I don't think so," said Blanche."

Don Rafa had brought out a bottle of tequila, poured out three glasses: "Never forget they used to bottle it in the same bottle as their cattle purge. Dozens of accidents. Ah, well you've heard that story…."

"She has to go, Willi, you see that?" Carl said. to Willi.

"Yes."

"She's sick. She's had too much. 'It's death,' she said; 'There's death here." She started saying it a month ago, when the hens were dying, now this…"

"Of course. It's their ways, Carl. There's an ancient balance."

Carl could hear the murmured *Salve Marias* from the cottage, and see the shadowy figure of *doña* Luz moving about the bed. The child was lying on the kitchen table, he could see, on top of a white tablecloth. The priest's voice was a rumbling counter bass.

"Goodbye, then. You will see, you will see, as my Cousin Bernardo says, The best starting out place, the best starting out place is aboard an international flight at…ah, well, you've heard that, yes, yes. My wife will regret…but as you see, she is busy with the necessary…and so, good luck to you. Unfortunate, what's happened, but she'll have another. Strong girl like her, how she did yell."

Chapter 5

Carl continued to care for the cow after Orlando left. He took on the extra jobs of milking, which took him twice as long as it had Orlando, and he also fed and hosed down the sow, who it seemed would not be having a litter despite her steady inflation. The male had been eaten at Christmas, so there were no prospects for more pigs, which suited *don* Rafa. Orlando's woman went about with a stoic energy caring for the chickens, and one of her sisters moved up to help with the washing.. The *Franceses* up the hill were invited to harvest the coffee crop. It was decided a night watchman was not needed as there was so little to steal, but Carl made one round of the wire fences at eleven o'clock just before he went to bed. The *Doña's margaritas* bloomed wildly after the rains, and the woodrose vine climbed over the roof. Carl and the *Doña* had finished the Henry Adams and were reading *Bleak House*.

His daytime chores were usually done by noon, when he took a shower and changed into clean clothes that Orlando's woman brought in and put on his bed every day. One of the reasons she was shy and confused around him, he decided, was that he spent all his afternoons at the big house, as if he had been a guest from the city. It was as if his slopping around with the pig was some sort of aberration only a gringo would indulge in.

She did little things like hanging a curtain in his kitchen, and when there were embers from her woodstove on baking day, she would fill the old-fashioned iron with them and press one of his better shirts as if to nudge him up to the level where he belonged.

AFTER CARL HAD DONE HIS SHOPPING in Tuxpan, Mondays, he continued on the bus, past the *abasto*, up the mountain to the margin of

Sergio and Sonia's property where Willi was living in an outbuilding that had been a goat shelter. There were only a few items that Willi needed from the town. A carton of Polar Beer, one pack of cigarettes—he smoked one cigarette each evening—salt, matches. For the rest, Willi had Sonia's chickens and the vegetable garden.

"Any news," Carl would ask, and there would be a hint by way of the pharmacist that the children had found their way to a caretaking family, of a plan being conceived. Finally there was confirmed information of another kidnapping in a distant province, intended as a swap for the mother's freedom. Sergio would never be freed.

Willi was holding the property together for Sonia. Weeding her garden and keeping her hens and harvesting some coffee which Carl would eventually sell in Tuxpan and the money would be put into an account for Sonia to have when she was free.

And he had found clay in the cut the backhoe had carved out of the mountainside to link up a new farmhouse to the main road. He showed it to Carl, wonderful shades of terra cotta and cream and lilac shoveled into plastic tubs; and a pile of sunbaked bricks, he was making in a wooden mold. First he would build a wood-fired oven, then he would bake bricks, then build a proper kiln. He would build himself a studio then and make sculptures from the same clay, the idea of them already in his head.

"Like the first man," Carl had said.

"Yeah, soon I won't need the cigarettes. I'm weaning myself."

And all the time, Carl knew, that Willi, who always did several things at once, was of course 'shouldering a rifle for Chu Teh.' But they never spoke of it beyond the news of the family.

"THAT FLAN HAS A NICE FACE," said don Rafa, wiping the corners of his mouth as Miriam removed the plates and Olga came behind with the tray of desserts.

"So, have you seen your painter friend?". He asked Carl.

Carl was cautious. "Not for a week."

"Is there any hope?" asked the Doña.

"Well, yes there might be," Carl said.

"We won't ask you for details," said don Rafa.

"There are people trying to move the government." Carl said.

"Yes, I can imagine how." said Rafa. And your friend?"

"He is harvesting Sergio's coffee," Carl said. "And living nearby."

Don Rafa had read of the new kidnapping in the newspaper, but Carl wouldn't be drawn into discussing it. Whatever its results, they would read of it in the paper. Don Rafa and the Doña would not be associated with anything Willi did in the future. Nor would Carl. He had told her one day as they walked on the garden paths about Sonia's request for her to help the children. He asked her if she would have done it. She had looked confused and said she would have had to think about it and take it up with the family. The following day, she had turned her wonderful gaze on him and brought it up again.

Yes, she would have done it, she told him. She could not have refused. They were innocent children, and Sonia was a good woman.

"And if someday Sonia is released?" he asked.

"I will take her to me," she told him.

Olga brought the after dinner infusion in the small cups that had belonged to don Rafa's mother. Doña Luz had picked manzanilla today from the little herb garden she kept in the center of the courtyard. Tomorrow there would be limoncillo or mint, to aid digestion. The rains started right after they finished lunch, and they separated to nap under wool blankets, to rise again at three for the Doña's lesson.

One thing Carl wondered as they took up Bleak House in the following month was if she had known that he and Blanche had not been married would she have made them marry, just as she had made Orlando marry Miriam. Probably not. They had still not been properly introduced at the time. Someday perhaps. Meanwhile he was watching.

About the Author

Barbara de la Cuesta lived in both Colombia and Venezuela. She has taught Spanish and is currently teaching English as a Second Language.

Her first novel, *The Spanish Teacher*, won The Gival Press Novel Award in 2007 and was published that year. She has also published a long poem, *If there Weren't So Many of Them* (BirchBrook Press, Delhi, N.Y. 1990 and Westerly, Professional Publishing Co., Dallas TX, 1994), a work of nonfiction in the field of arts therapy, as well as stories in the California Quarterly, and the Texas Review.

She received a fiction fellowship from the Massachusetts Artists Foundation and more recently a fiction fellowship from the New Jersey Council on the Arts. She was also given a Geraldine Dodge fellowship to the Virginia Center, in 2002 and a fellowship to the Millay Colony in 2008.